THE EMANCIPATION OF B

I think the book is wonderful. Vivid and absorbing and thought-provoking... [B] is an odd character, yes, but I found myself really caring what became of him. Chapeau, as they say in France!
Tony Peake, author of *A Summer Tide*, *Son to the Father*, *Seduction* and a biography of Derek Jarman

I finished the book over the weekend, and was completely hooked all the way through. You are a marvellous writer, observer, and guide. You said the narrative would reveal itself slowly, which it did, but to have kept the reader's attention when sometimes we were witnessing quite humdrum events in quite ordinary lives, is a tribute to your skill. You simply had to turn the page! ...Your descriptions of the nuances of childhood and family dissonance are absolutely spot on. I think the book is both haunting and memorable and I salute you for it.
Laura Morris, literary agent

A hymn to mindfulness and a moving meditation on our conflicting ideas of home in a novel that explores one solitary man's efforts to find sanctuary in the most unlikely of places.
Paul Wilson, author of *The Visiting Angel*

The
Emancipation
of B

The Emancipation of B

Jennifer Kavanagh

Winchester, UK
Washington, USA

First published by Roundfire Books, 2015
Roundfire Books is an imprint of John Hunt Publishing Ltd., Laurel House, Station Approach,
Alresford, Hants, SO24 9JH, UK
office1@jhpbooks.net
www.johnhuntpublishing.com
www.roundfire-books.com

For distributor details and how to order please visit the 'Ordering' section on our website.

Text copyright: Jennifer Kavanagh 2014

ISBN: 978 1 78279 884 2

A CIP catalogue record for this book is available from the British Library.

Design: Stuart Davies

Printed in the USA by Edwards Brothers Malloy

We operate a distinctive and ethical publishing philosophy in all
areas of our business, from our global network of authors to
production and worldwide distribution.

By the same author

The Methuen Book of Animal Tales (ed.)
The Methuen Book of Humorous Stories (ed.)
Call of the Bell Bird
The World is our Cloister
New Light (ed.)
Journey Home (formerly The O of Home)
Simplicity Made Easy
Small Change, Big Deal
The Failure of Success

Acknowledgements

I'd like to thank Natalie Cronin, Jalkirty Rawal, Kenneth Scott and Catherine Woodman, for the generous sharing of their expertise. Any mistakes are mine.

I'd also like to give thanks to Tony Peake and Laura Morris whose faith in the book gave me the courage to go on.

Chapter 1

B knew that he had begun to talk to himself. Although the walls were thick, he was always worried that he might betray himself. So, whenever he caught himself at it, he was careful, just in case some sharp-eared brat might hear him.

- I heard a voice, Mum, I did. I'm not making it up. A man's voice.

- Don't be silly, dear, that's an empty building. Look at it, all falling down.

No, it was all right. No one knew he was there and that was how he liked it.

The building was at the end of a cul de sac: on the corner, really, with a pointy bit at the rear where office blocks from roads on either side converged. So the view out the back was entirely brick and concrete, but with a miraculous dip at the end, revealing sky. He was completely un-overlooked on that side, and had been able to clean the sash window, inside and out, and open the bottom to allow air into the room. This window was his special delight, looking, as it did, on to a light-well into which no human could intrude. It was still: immune, it seemed, to weather of any kind. Prison-like, yes, but a cell of his own choosing and, as in a prison, the smallest sign of beauty was magnified: the stars, a cloud, even a pigeon flying over. And the walls were of old London brick, textured, mottled beige, brown, verging on the black. It was not a space into which direct sun entered – for that he had to go to the front – but it was his own outdoor space. He could, without fear of being observed, hobble to the window and lay aside his crutches, standing alone and naked to the world.

That morning, the flickering yellow light on the wall opposite had woken him as usual, when the rubbish lorry made its twice-daily collection. It was one of the benefits of living in a trading area. That, and the street sweepers: two shifts a day of orange-jacketed men, each with broom, shovel and wheelie-bin. The whispering sound of brush on pavement was often the first sound that roused him in the morning, a sound so delicate – so old fashioned – it was a reassuring reminder of the possibility of an ordered world.

He'd woken, as he often did, with a strong sense of his youthful self. Strange how, no matter how many years passed, no matter what happened, that self-image remained constant. He remembered an old science teacher at school (well, he was probably about fifty, but he was ancient to them) saying: "I don't feel a day older than you lot," and the horror, pity and rolling eyes that had greeted this astonishing remark. What was he on? But, now B, still quite young, admittedly, understood that teacher: B still saw himself as that tousle-headed schoolboy with strong sturdy limbs, pink and blotchy from exertion in his running shorts. Chunky, muscular legs that would bear anything. The act of getting out of bed and meeting the challenges of the day soon reminded him of how out of date that image was.

B had been a pretty little boy with blonde curls that his mother said were the envy of her friends. But he was also a sulky child. Photos of him as young as four or five showed him with a downturned mouth, his eyes usually turned away from the camera, as if in search of a world better than the one in front of him. He had always been wary of photos, felt somehow that the person wielding the camera had some power over him. But the bad temper visible in the photos was not only about his unwillingness to be there, but a reflection of his attitude to life generally. He suffered the tasks imposed on him by his mother to help her – hanging out the washing, emptying the rubbish – with an ill grace. Why me? his expression said. And the answer was always: because there's no one else. Annette was always away; his father either at work or, later on, impeded by arthritic joints. Dad had not complained – indeed he was a largely silent man – but getting about had become increasingly difficult for him as B got older. And B, whatever his inclinations, was strong and capable.

In those early photos, too, B's eyes were screwed up, as if against the sun. It hadn't been until he was about three that they realised that he was not dim but acutely short-sighted. But somehow they had never got out of the habit of treating him as if he were indeed stupid, and he came to believe it. He could not, after all, hope to compete with the charisma of his sister.

His parents were old when he was born – old and tired – and it was not their idea of fun to be faced with a dreamy child who from an early age had had to wear glasses, and whose clumsiness threatened the painstakingly acquired treasures of their home. The only time his mother had hit him – it was like a bombshell, and a traumatic memory to this day – was when he had backed into the spindly little tea table and broken its leg. He couldn't understand why a little table, a pretty useless little thing, after all, should matter so much.

Annette had been twelve when B arrived, and away at university by the time he was six. It was like being an only child. They had never been close. She was bright, charming, frivolous – everything he wasn't – and after so many years his parents had found it hard to adjust to his vague and increasingly sullen presence. Annette could jolly them out of their weariness; he just seemed to add to it. He felt as if he was trapped in a dark corner while the sunshine passed him by.

When his sister was away, family life was pretty dull. The three of them sat at supper with little to say to each other. Between delicately forked mouthfuls, Mother would speak a little about her church activities, what people were wearing, and the escalating cost of food. Dad knew better than to bore her with his work goings-on, and B was usually silent. It was the best option when opening his mouth so often exposed him to scorn or ridicule. The tension as they ate made B long for the sanctuary of his room.

It was only when Annette came back from uni that the place lit up. For days before her arrival, Mother was energised, getting in food that she knew Annette particularly liked, cleaning the house to an even more sparkling shine. Once Annette arrived, the phone rang, her friends popped in, and Annette herself was full of her activities, regaling them all at dinner with stories that felt to B as if they'd come from a distant land.

When he was small, the teenage girls that filled the house terrified him – they were big, loud and unpredictable. Above all, they wanted him as a plaything and, from a very early age, everything in him rejected this role. Annette in particular wouldn't leave him alone. When B wouldn't react to her teasing – didn't really understand it – it was as if Annette had to get under his skin in some other way, so she nosed about in his room: the one thing that she knew would really get to him. He was private; she didn't know what made him tick, and he was very sure he would not allow her to find out. He kept his own counsel: his power was in that. No one knew what he was thinking or feeling. No one knew him, or what mattered. It was a lonely existence, true, but no one could get at him in any way that was significant. When he was about seven, he saved up his pocket money to buy a lock, so that she couldn't get into his private space. It was *his*.

Pocket money was a God-send. Yes, B liked the feel of money in his hand. But it was not so much for what he wanted to buy – there wasn't much – but for the feeling of power it gave him. Having control over one little corner of his life. Something that was his, and that no one could take away. It was his father who gave the money to him every Saturday morning: a quid to begin with, moving up a bit as he got older. B imagined his parents were fair – he occasionally heard what others got – but he wasn't much bothered. What did matter was the regular meeting with his dad, and the fact that it was he that gave him the money. It was something that brought them together and gave them an opportunity to talk, although in general little was actually said. There was some debate about when the weekly tip should stop. At eighteen – *you're an adult now* – it did.

As a family they didn't mix much. Apart from Annette, who was untypically gregarious. Mother had her church cronies and his father had work colleagues, and that seemed to be enough. *We keep ourselves to ourselves.* The local population had become much more diverse in the years that B's parents had lived there. Mother didn't like it, and could be heard muttering darkly about falling house prices, and how the neighbourhood was going downhill. She didn't think much of their neighbours anyhow – on one side the Wellands whose rows often woke her at night and, on the other, the over-sociable Enid, whose origins were uncertain and her accent beyond the pale. As for the *coloured people* whose garden backed on to theirs,

- *Black, Mother.*
- *They're not black, they're brown.* There was no telling her.

Mother had written to the council again and again about their bonfires that she said dirtied her washing. *Look at the smuts on my nightie, B. Now I'll have to wash it all over again.*

There wasn't much extended family. Dad was from Leeds, and his brother still lived there. The wives didn't really get on, so the families didn't see much of each other. Annette, though, social being that she was, was keen to keep up the family connection, so from time to time they trundled up the A1 for a tea party of stultifying boredom. B did, however, feel some kinship with his cousin Angus. On one occasion, fleeing outside "for a breath of fresh air", B had encountered him in the garden, on a similar mission. They had growled at each other, then retreated, leaving each other peaceably alone.

B was a solitary child. Withdrawal was a habit from an early age and people soon lost patience with trying to draw him out. His was an escapist mentality. He had a yearning for the outside world that took him, as no more than a toddler, to disappearing off, out of the house, whenever Mother wasn't looking. Houses, for him, were no more than shelter; the real world was outside. Even at night, after he had gone to bed, he knelt on his bed, pulled aside the curtain and gazed out hungrily at the moon and the stars, as if willing them to reveal their secrets. But during the day he could escape into the haven of the garden, with its birds and butterflies, squirrels, and even the occasional fox. To his bewilderment, most animals fled when he emerged from the house, but he contented himself by scrabbling around on the ground, watching the busyness of all the insects that were hardly visible when standing from even his diminutive height.

Mother had a horror of wildlife of any kind: despite B's pleading, there had been no possibility of bringing any of the school animals home for the holidays. She spent a good deal of her time eradicating any creaturely trace from the house: swatting flies, squashing moths, and brushing the shiny wonder of cobwebs away with a peremptory broom. She protected the margins of the house by putting ant powder outside near the doors, and attempted to sterilise even the garden itself, with snail pellets and rat poison. She would not allow any feeding of the birds for fear of rats. *There's plenty for the birds to eat, B, and anyway, it'll be the pigeons who'll take it all.*

When Mother finally persuaded his father to replace the grass with a geometric pattern of paving slabs, B thought that all was lost, but after a while he found that the creatures would not be defeated, and with delight noted the appearance of worms, slugs and beetles from under the slabs at the edges of the flower beds and even, eventually, from the spaces in between. Mother never knew about the hedgehog that he kept warm through the winter near the compost heap in the corner, nor about the insects smuggled into the house in matchboxes. Though she did complain about loose matches in the kitchen drawer with nothing to strike them on. Eventually, when putting his shorts out to be washed, he carelessly left a matchbox in one of the pockets, and all was discovered.

B had always felt more at ease with animals, and had loved Jeff, the cocker spaniel they'd had at home, who was not his, specifically, but he was sure they had a special bond. He loved the trusting brown eyes on his, the simplicity of the dog's affections and reactions – to food, walks, just to B's company, it seemed. It melted his heart. He could welcome in Jeff what he couldn't accept in any other living being: his physicality, the heat of the dog's body against his, his nuzzling and slobbering; he felt an uncomplicated warmth of loving for Jeff that he'd never felt with humans. People were just so bloody difficult. When Jeff was run over, even at a ripe old age when semi-blindness had driven him into the path of a car, something in B had died, and one of the things he could not forgive his mother for was that she would not allow him to get another dog. She'd never really liked Jeff, but had given in when Annette as a little girl had had a passing fancy for a puppy. Once Annette had left home, there was no way Mother would allow another smelly animal to cross her threshold. *I know who would have to look after it, feed it and clear up its messes, and it wouldn't be you, would it?* Dad, who B hoped might plead his cause, had been, as usual when it mattered, away on a job.

B's father was often away. His heating business took him all over the place, and at all hours. In his late teens, he'd been invited down by a friend to join a new central heating firm, and he'd stayed down in London ever since. It was when he was doing a job in the area that he'd met Mother "across the counter" at the local pharmacy where she'd worked until she left to have Annette. Over the years Dad had built up a loyal clientele and a good reputation so, soon after they bought their home, he decided to set up on his own. Work was plentiful, and he was highly regarded. Being self-employed had its benefits: there was flexibility of hours; he could please himself. Later, as the economy shrank, money became tight, and he had to work long hours to keep the business afloat. Except at the top end, people drew in their horns during a recession.

The Emancipation of B

B had always had a sensitivity to buildings, had felt uncomfortable or ill at ease in a space itself, regardless of who lived there. When he was small, Annette had scoffed at his discomfort during a visit to a neighbour, as he pulled at her hand to take him away. He couldn't have said why – the old man was kind enough – but there was something in the place that made B need to leave. He had never felt at ease in their own house either, though it was his mother's pride and joy. She was especially proud that it was theirs, having taken advantage in the eighties of the newly established right to buy. B didn't know why he didn't like it, but now, with the wisdom of distance, he thought it a mean little dwelling, with thin partitions easily penetrated by their neighbours' telly and rows, and low ceilings that blotted out the sky. Like the others in the street, it was fortified with heavy locks on the front door and bars on the ground-floor windows. It was a house that had been the scene of his constraint and had never felt like home. How could he have felt happy there? But now, in this space, in these two rooms, he had from the beginning felt at peace. Of course a lot had to do with the fruition of his dream, the culmination of years of planning, but it was more than that. These high-ceilinged rooms, for all their dirt and dilapidation, were *all right*. This was a space that let him breathe, seemed to contribute to a healing process. He felt it in his bones.

B had no idea who had lived there before – it had obviously been some time since the last people had left. Had they fallen on hard times? The furniture left behind was pretty ragged, but they had presumably taken the best stuff with them. What had they been like, these people who had chosen, and had been able to afford, to live in the middle of a city like this? The atmosphere was so benign that he felt he might have liked them. Certainly there was no threat emanating from these walls. Reassurance, rather. Goodness knows what would have happened if it had been different. After years of expecting – and usually getting – the worst, fear seemed to have gone out of the door the moment he had come in here, the moment he had claimed life for himself. He was no longer squashed, subject; he was free; he was, however disabled, alive.

In the front room, where he slept, B had had to let the grime on the window remain. He still had his own peep holes but from the outside this part of the building was as battered and forlorn as all the rest. The crumbling of some part of the upper building had left a film of dust on the window, smeared into opaqueness by the wind and rain. He was unobserved.

Nonetheless, B limited the time that he spent looking out of the front window. The rooms were of a womb-like quality that suited his aspiration to an interior life. So his exposure to the outside world was quite deliberate, a "walk" that he took before and after "work": after breakfast once he was dressed, and before preparing supper and settling down for the evening. Even through the murk the aspect was bright and airy, with a clear run up the road and few cars passing, except to turn round the little island at the end of the road in front of him. And on that traffic island there were two trees, twin sentinels of the natural world.

B was often surprised by what met his eyes through the peep holes: the weather, in particular, of which he had little inkling from the thick-walled rooms, apart from the length of sunlight. From the centre of the city, it was hard to keep track of subtle seasonal changes, but they were marked by the human as well as by the plant population. He found that he relied quite a bit on what people outside were wearing. As trees shed their covering of leaves, baring their branches to the sky, human beings covered up their nakedness with more and more layers, culminating in coats and hats and scarves and boots. On a few days there was a sprinkling of snow: a shiny bright presence until trodden into a slimy beige slush.

On sunny days, B took pleasure in the sharp shadows cast by one building on another: the clear-cut shades of red and brown bricks in the sun. If there was a strong wind, he could tell it only from the bowing of the trees in the distance or as people in the street below hung on to their hats and struggled to keep upright. He enjoyed this microcosm of city life. A couple of times, among people on their mobile phones, or jogging along the road, he caught sight of an empty rickshaw: such a strangely unexpected sight on a modern London street. Sometimes maps, knapsacks and un-English gesticulation identified passers-by as tourists who had wandered off the beaten track.

B was struck by the free and easy way in which people went on their way. Where did they get their confidence from? Was it all a big show, hiding the same insecurity as his own, or did they really – these men in suits, women in heels, groups of laughing young people – did they feel at ease in the world, with each other and among strangers? Where did they get the assurance? They didn't teach it in any school he'd been to.

This wasn't a family area. B never saw children, or even dogs, which saddened him. Probably in the flats round about, no pets were allowed. Most people that he saw were purposeful, on their way somewhere, but there was a core of regulars, who presumably lived near by.

Although he had never left the building and no one knew he was there, B felt very much a part of the neighbourhood. He knew nothing of what lay beyond what he could actually see, but even as a silent spectator he felt he was part of the street scene, a witness to its regular comings and goings. The difference here was that these people could have no consciousness of being watched. He could not affect their behaviour. What he was seeing was their natural, raw state. He did not feel a voyeur because he didn't feel outside their life. The familiarity of their presence gave him a comfortable sense of belonging.

For instance, there was Bert. B gave the regulars names, as he saw them so often that he felt he knew them. It was a one-way acquaintance, of course, since they had never to his knowledge seen him. Bert was a broad squat man who donned a peak cap in cold weather. His job seemed to consist of pushing large wheelie bins into the entrance of the block of flats opposite. B supposed that he was some sort of caretaker, though he never saw him do anything other than push the bins. But he was cheery, often greeting passers-by with a wave and a grin – and his presence brightened up the street.

Another of the regulars, Maud, as he liked to call her, generally appeared during his morning "stroll". She had a pale broad face and was, he guessed, pretty elderly. She always wore white socks and flat shoes, and walked with legs far apart, generally dressed in close-fitting clothes that did her lumpy figure no favours. Maud liked to feed the pigeons, much to the displeasure of one or two of the street sweepers, who generally swept up the bread once she had disappeared.

On the corner across the road, almost directly opposite the front window, was a building site. Not a gaping hole, but a scaffolded building, Victorian, like the one he was in, but three times the width: a grand house that was being renovated with meticulous care. The work had gone on for months, and he watched the comings and goings with interest, especially at the beginning, when they put the scaffolding up: men in helmets and bare well-muscled arms climbing athletically from one level to another. Outside, at lunchtime on sunny days, a line of men sat on the ground (*germs, B*) in their overalls, on their mobiles, eating lunch, grouped, in pairs, or alone, staring into the distance. Some of them were probably the same sort of age as himself, but he envied them their fitness, their physical activity: they had a hearty appetite, he had no doubt, and no problem sleeping. He imagined them going home at the end of the day, maybe to somewhere cheaper outside London, to wife and children. Family life, shoes off, a shower, a meal cooked, a drink in hand in front of the telly. And on the days when they were not to be seen, he knew it was the weekend, probably a Sunday. How seductively familiar their routines were, how hard it was to remove himself entirely from such worldly patterns.

Sundays had never meant much to him. His mother had always attended the local parish church: a large Victorian red-brick edifice, built at a time when congregations were larger than the twenty-five or so that gathered these days for the weekly service. To begin with, he had been dragged to Sunday School. The woman who ran it was nice enough, a bit scatty, and quite content to have a child who didn't cry when his parents left, or have to restrain from running into the main body of the church during the service. Who was content, indeed, with the tattered old books they'd never had the time or money to replace. But B preferred to spend the time at his gran's and, after a while, realising that his father didn't go to church, B dug in his heels and eventually got his way.

Gran's house was a haven. She lived just up the road, so it was easy for him to escape not only on Sunday mornings but after school, and she was always undemandingly pleased to see him, the biscuit tin always full. She was tiny, but then, he supposed, most old women were. Even though he himself was little, he had felt like a cart horse beside her, but she never made him feel it. How he wished she'd lived. He felt a rare tenderness as he thought of her, and imagined walking with her to the corner shop, she tucking her arm confidentially in his, and smiling up at him as he bent to talk into her better ear. Granddad had died before he was born, but he could tell from the way Gran talked about him, with such wistfulness and such admiration, that they had been very much in love.

B's special place was the attic room in Gran's house. He often thought now of the sanctuary of that windowless, un-overlooked room, felt that he had perhaps re-created it in these rooms – created the same sense of security and anonymity; the right to be himself with no prying eyes. He didn't remember his sister ever taking any notice of the attic. Indeed, she preferred the telly, and couldn't generally be bothered to go round to see their gran.

In that attic room was a box of childish toys, which were mostly beneath his notice, and a few dog-eared books, which he treasured. Those books with their lovely musty old smell held many of the secrets of his childhood: *The Red Book of Heroes*, all those books of fairy tales, but especially *King Arthur and his Knights of the Round Table*. It was a hardback with rounded softened corners to its cover and brightly coloured plates that transported him to another land. It was not Lancelot – that traitor to his king – who caught his attention, but some of the lesser knights. Sir Percevale, in particular, who was brought up wild in the forest, with no knowledge of chivalry, and generally thought a fool. He could relate to that. Percevale was one of three knights who found the grail and lived. One drawback was that his sister was the bearer of the grail – they got that wrong; that could never happen. But Percevale fell in love, yes, he fell in love. And that, for twelve-year-old B, was a prophecy; it touched his heart; he knew it to be true for Sir Percevale, and, secretly, for himself.

The church was the centre of his mother's social life. Here, rather than among their neighbours, were people *of our sort* and she had made some friends. Organising fundraising activities quite often took her out at weekends, and on the occasional evening, times when B (and, he fondly imagined, his father) could breathe a little. But his mother's religious life – if that was what it was – impinged on the household only to the extent of a brief grace before meals, which B, who enjoyed his food, found harmless enough. Religion itself wasn't discussed. God was not acknowledged. Any questions from B were treated as unseemly by his mother and met with non-committal noises from his father, who didn't want to put his children off something which, even if not to his own liking, he considered generally "a good thing".

For his father, Sundays were for fishing. That was his place of solitude and silence, away from the demands of work and family. As a small child, B had gone with him on just one precious occasion. It was vivid in his mind, although he didn't remember why he'd been allowed to go. Maybe Mother had had something on after church and Gran wasn't free, or maybe his father had just relented in the face of B's earnest longing. They left early in the morning (Mother was still in her dressing gown) wrapped up against the rain, with a thermos, sandwiches and cake. They had gone in the car – a rare treat – packing the boot with rods, umbrella and wellington boots. B was thrilled to be spending a day alone with his father, and excitement had kept him awake for much of the previous night.

Most of the day had indeed been a joy, sitting in silence by the river, remembering what he'd been told about keeping still, and trying to not to look at the mass of maggots wriggling in the bottom of the pail. Instead, he concentrated on watching the slow-moving water, and listening to the gurgling as it tumbled over the stones underneath. It was calm and cool in the early morning, and the peace of the place seemed to seep into the very core of him. As he considered the day stretching ahead, he felt a rare ease and contentment. His father sat motionless for the most part, staring into space, just occasionally lifting his rod and flicking the line back into the water. But when his father caught a fish – *Don't worry, B, I always throw them back* – the sight of the poor little thing squirming on the end of the line with a hook in its mouth upset B so much that they'd had to come home. His father packed up the car and drove back in tight-lipped silence. B had never gone again.

He was, he knew, a disappointment to his father. When he was born, so many years after Annette, he imagined that his father had rejoiced at the idea of a son. But B was not the sort of son Dad would have longed for. They had both known it, and it was a sadness to B that he could not find in himself something that would create a bond with his father. He was not the kind of son who would join his father and friends in the pub, nor one who found pleasure in making things. Early attempts at helping his father make a set of bookshelves were a disaster: he simply didn't have the patience or the co-ordination. He wasn't practical. Nor was Annette, for that matter, but no one expected it of girls. B simply didn't fit in; he didn't relate to the world: not to his family in which he'd always felt an outsider, and certainly not to anybody at school.

It was a former grammar school with uniform and pretensions. It was of course single-sex, as Mother viewed the mingling of impressionable boys and girls with suspicion and even Dad agreed, feeling that girls might be a distraction. B could sense that his parents had braced themselves against a tirade of refusal, and that they were somewhat relieved to find that he didn't object. Secretly, it was a relief for him too; girls scared him even more than boys. He knew what it was to be a boy, and everything he'd seen of Annette and her friends showed them to be an alien species.

But even with the boys he hadn't fitted in. They hadn't known what to make of him. B was not a child of his time. Apart from anything else, the electronic revolution had largely passed him by. While he envied other socially inept boys who lost themselves in the internet, his own interest was limited. He wasn't technologically minded, and had never been very interested in facts – perhaps the reason he floundered academically. He didn't have the necessary intellectual curiosity. But he did want to know a little more about things that mattered to him, to confirm understanding that came from his own experience. So although computers didn't interest him in themselves, and he didn't yearn for one of his own, he did check things out on the one in the local library. It was in any case always good to find a way of being away from the house.

B wasn't a swot – that was in his favour – but he shared none of the interests of the other boys, and refused to join in the largely filthy banter in the playground. Well, they would have taken it as a refusal, but the fact was, he simply didn't understand it.

One day stood out from all those dreary days at school. He had missed out on the trip to the zoo, because he'd been at home with a cold when they were taking names for it. Mother would have objected to the cost, he imagined, and in any case, although he longed for an opportunity to spend time with animals, he wasn't sure he could have borne the sight of them all cooped up. But he did go on the trip to the British Library. He wasn't particularly keen on the idea to begin with, but any day out of school was a bonus.

That term, the art classes had been focused on calligraphy, creating art through writing, something which B had found intensely frustrating. Although he loved the intricacies of others' drawings – the fine lines, the patterns of ancient motifs – he himself smudged the ink and simply couldn't get the lines where he wanted them. But he paid attention, partly out of interest, and partly because Mr Pocock, an elderly podgy little man, with chins that wobbled, took an interest in him. As B had little co-ordination and less technique, he was surprised to hear that Mr P felt he had something. His teacher talked of how in a quick sketch B sometimes got the feel of a person, the mood of a place. Though the others took the mickey of the funny little man, B had treasured such a rare glimmer of connection.

And it was to an exhibition of illuminated manuscripts that Mr Pocock took them that day. B was enchanted. While other boys lounged about, scuffing their heels on the floor, eyeing up any passing girls, B's short-sighted eyes were glued to the manuscripts, to those extraordinarily ornate capital letters. The lines were ornamented with swirls and twirls, leaves and flowers, some of them reaching way out beyond the letter itself. And the "empty" spaces in the letters were filled with people, animals, even a snake. He was, of course, particularly drawn to the capital Bs. He was arrested by a particular letter B with St Bernard: a full figure standing in the letter, his arm resting on the horizontal divide between the two halves, his face half-turned to the reader. Such a humane face. Not all the manuscripts, B was surprised to see, were religious. Yes, some of the most beautiful pages were from Bibles, but there were medical books, calendars – all sorts of things, including ones about animals – bestiaries, as they were called. All sorts of amazing-looking creatures.

And then his heart jolted as his eyes lit on *The Romance of Lancelot du Lac*. There were his beloved knights! The book was open at the moment when Lancelot met Guinevere – not a moment that B wanted to remember. But, maybe there were scenes with others in them, maybe even Percevale.

B swallowed. Revealing anything of his dream-life was anathema, but today his excitement was such that he could not resist expressing it, even at the risk of disclosure. So, he approached his teacher in what he hoped was a casual manner.

- *Erm, Mr Pocock?*

- *Yes, my boy?*

- *Erm, I like... I mean, are there...? Do you think I could see...?*

Pleased at this sign of interest, Mr P smiled down at him benignly and said, *Do you mean other pages of this book?*

- *Yes. Yes, that's right. Please.*

Mr P strolled over to a curator, who showed them to a machine in the corner on which they could scroll down to look at other images of any of the exhibits. Breathing quickly, his mouth dry, B followed the links, and soon found himself in front of an image of Perceval (they spelt it without an "e"), and Galahad praying. B couldn't tell which of the two was his hero. They were both wearing helmets, and squeezed into the tininess of the letter O they looked much the same. Another picture showed the two knights with one called Bohort of whom B had never heard, looking at a sword on a bed. With them was "a damsel". B took a keen look, but again she was too tiny, indeed only roughly drawn – sadly, nothing to write home about, not someone to capture his heart.

B was an outsider, yes, but he was never bullied. He'd had an energy – a fierceness? – that held others at bay. He might have been dreamy, but he was big and strong: not someone to tangle with, perhaps. He'd only been violent once at school, and still remembered the sensation of fist on cheek, his painful bloody knuckles. He still shuddered at the shockingly pleasurable feeling as bone crunched through flesh, as the boy went down and the others backed off. Apart from the odd bit of half-hearted name-calling – *four-eyes* – there had never been any trouble afterwards. Stories and embroidered myth travelled fast. And, though he had a temper, he worked hard to keep it under control. He knew that he never again wanted to hit another human being. It was too dangerously delicious.

His one pleasure at school was running. It was lucky that they did cross-country, in the winter at least. B was no good at ball games: his eyesight and co-ordination weren't up to it, so he had opted out of the whole football culture – another black mark on his street cred. But for running he had the stamina. He wasn't thin and wiry like the best long-distance runners, but his sturdy legs kept going. And it was a gloriously solitary activity in a world oppressed by other boys. There were still the showers to negotiate, but for one glorious afternoon a week he was out on his own, sniffing the air, pawing the earth, keeping his body fit.

The need to run extended beyond that one winter afternoon a week. Telling his parents that his PE teacher had told him to train, he went out in the early morning at weekends. He wasn't allowed to go out in the dark, so could only run after school once the days got longer. It wasn't just the freedom – which was exhilarating – but the licence to get filthy. Running through mud was a special delight, the squidging beneath his trainers (the idea of running barefoot was an almost unbearably erotic dream), the spattering, the carelessness about the condition of himself and his clothes. Sheer sensuous joy! Mother complained, of course, at the state of him, but although maybe the shower did get a bit mucky, he didn't really see what she had to moan about. She had a washing machine, didn't she? And he cleaned his shoes himself.

B had continued the practice into adult life. There was no need for any organisation; he could just pull on a tracksuit or shorts, shut the door and go – round the park, down to the reservoir, whatever, revelling in the freedom, the rain, the mud, and the greenness of grass and trees all around him. And the rhythm, the rhythm that put everything back in its place.

B's principal memory of his teenage years was of being dragged from one function to another, with polished shoes, jacket and tie, in a state of mute boredom. Uncle Harry's birthday, Annette and Rob's wedding, of course – in white, natch, though he had serious doubts about that. Rob seemed a nice enough man, though B knew little about him except that he was in "estate management", whatever that meant. B supposed it had something to do with managing the lands of some wealthy farmer. In any case, they seemed well enough off.

At these events, apart from the children, with whom he often had to sit, B was always the youngest. When his father and Rob joined the other men in going outside the back door for a smoke, he longed to join them, but even when he escaped the clutches of Mother he never felt part of the group; he was never taken seriously, though his father tried to be kind. The talk was generally of politics or cars, and he knew little of either.

The family usually gathered for birthdays. B didn't even enjoy his own, feeling that any idea of celebration was pretty pointless. After Gran died, who would truthfully celebrate his existence? As for presents, what did anyone know of his tastes? Sometimes Dad would slip him a fiver to spend as he liked, but otherwise, the seemingly random choice of books and clothes made him squirm. At least after a few years Mother had stopped knitting for him. When he was little, she used to save money by using up any odds and ends of wool that she happened to have to hand, often in completely uncomplementary colours. Thank God that uniform had prevented him having to wear any of her creations at school. Apart from the swimming trunks, that was – a particularly painful memory. They were red and, when they got wet, they sagged.

B had dreaded the annual suggestion of a party. *No, honestly, Mother, I'd rather not.* Whom would he have invited? When it became apparent that there was no avoiding some kind of an event, after a few painful years B had managed to establish the tradition of a family picnic. It was the right time of year, after all, and a combination of food and the open air made up for the enforced gathering of the clan. Mother made his favourite lemonade and seemed to make an effort to provide food that he liked and, with an even greater effort, not to make a comment about the inadequacy of his diet. As an adult, he'd come round to the idea of having a special day just for him, but it had to be on his own terms, and when and where he chose.

When B was about seventeen, one of Mother's church friends provided an unexpected opportunity for escape. Lynn and Andrew were a middle-aged couple with no children and two beloved cats. They were keen on foreign holidays, disliked putting their little dears in a cattery, and were always on the lookout for a trustworthy cat-sitter. One day they asked Mother if B might be available. Although she did not have great faith in B's ability to stay somewhere without messing it up, she had too much pride to confess her misgivings to anyone outside the family, or actively dissuade them from taking him on. And, besides, she was no doubt relieved to be shot of him for a while. B was delighted to make some money and to have the opportunity to spend some time away from the house, without the need to converse with anyone. He was especially pleased to have the company of animals, although in the event he found their cats on the snooty side. He preferred dogs.

It was an adventure, living somewhere else, among other

people's things. B didn't really listen when his mother talked about her friends, but he knew they both worked, and they obviously had a lot more money than his own family. The house was a big one, detached, with its own drive. They had glossy photos in silver frames on the sideboard, and china figures on the shelves. Some ornaments had obviously been bought abroad; coming from a family that never travelled, it brought a tinge of the exotic into B's life.

It was an eye-opener to see how they lived. Without close neighbours, their house was wonderfully quiet: he couldn't hear anyone from anywhere else. In the evenings, B lay on his back on the thick pile yellowish carpet (*get up, this instant, B!*), hands cupping his head, gazing at the subtly shifting bits of glass in the chandelier glinting rainbow-coloured in the light. This, he'd felt, was as good as it got.

The contrast with his present surroundings couldn't have been more stark. There was no way B would lie down on this floor, even if he could have reached it, which he no longer could. Even after his best efforts with a brush, he knew that the worn carpet would not bear close scrutiny – he couldn't even work out its original colour. It was sticky to the touch, which meant he was unable to walk barefoot, his usual indoor habit. Although he had done his best, sweeping the dust away from the corners, when he put his glasses on in the morning, or after meditation, the streaks on the walls and the stains on the floor came into sharper focus, and they weren't pretty. Maybe he was more his mother's child than he knew. There was, of course, no vacuum cleaner in the place, and, in any case, although the walls were thick enough, he wouldn't have risked the noise. But, for all the grubbiness of this place, the sense of freedom was the same as in Lynn and Andrew's posh house. Indeed, it was even greater, since it was permanent, it was "his", and no one could come and take it away.

Strangely, when B had lived with his family, in a house with all mod cons, when he was cooked for, his clothes washed and ironed, when he lacked for nothing in a material sense, his life had felt narrow and constrained. He'd been trapped in an existence that was not his own. Now, in conditions that most would consider inadequate, if not insanitary, B had expanded. He was living his life.

B didn't know where the idea of being a hermit came from. His parents never talked about religion, and the RE teacher at school had been pathetic – everyone played about in his classes. None of it seemed to mean anything. In fact, the whole idea of being a hermit didn't seem to have much to do with religion: it was more to do with solitude, though he remembered an image from the box of postcards in his grandparents' attic. Most were reproductions of famous paintings, some in black and white. The one of the hermit he remembered quite clearly: it was a rather grey picture of a small bearded head, partly turned towards the viewer, hands together in prayer – all that could be seen in the small window at the top of a tall thin tower. He couldn't remember who it was – St Antony, maybe? What a peaceful life, he remembered thinking, no one to make you do things. And someone to bring you food and so on – it sounded good, even then. And now he took some satisfaction in the fact that he might be growing to resemble that picture, in his beard, if nothing else, although his was of course not grey. Hermits had to be old, it seemed.

In his youth B had briefly had monastic leanings, had secretly begun to attend a different church from his mother's and had even explored the idea of taking instruction, but the concept of "stability" had made it clear that the monastic life was not for him. The idea of spending the rest of his life with the same group of people, *any* group of people, was abhorrent. Rubbing along with all those men. Where was the solitude, the stillness, in that? It was just the world made small, a microcosm of all he had always known and found so hard. And, surely, the original meaning of the word "monk" was a hermit, someone who lived in solitude. That was what he was after.

His foray into churchgoing was soon over. All that standing up and down, and reciting things written by someone else, much of which he simply didn't believe. He couldn't with sincerity mouth the creed, and as for turning to some bod next to him to bless them, that was the last straw. In church too he experienced the usual sinking feeling that he did not fit in. He felt hemmed in, couldn't wait to get out. He soon acknowledged that he did not have an orthodox faith in God, and that his longing did not have a specifically religious basis.

In many ways this place was perfect: it was entirely appropriate that an anchorite should dwell in the heart of a city. The silence here was extraordinary. Although at the front there was the occasional sound of a car, of people walking in the road, some indication of being in a city, in this room at the back all was still. There was no sign of any living creature. It tickled him to think that he could be hidden for so long in the centre of a city.

At first B thought he was seeing things, but on reflection he knew he was not mistaken. There was something strange going on in the house opposite. The previous day during his morning "walk", he had enjoyed watching one of the builders perched up there on the scaffolding, sitting astride a plank as he carefully painted round the intricate stonework of the window. Now, soon after sunrise, as B looked up to see what progress had been made, he saw a glint, a flash, as the early sun caught some movement within. It was soon gone, but B was sure he hadn't imagined it. Up there, on it must have been a fourth or fifth floor, in a building that was still a hard-hat area and had almost certainly been gutted, someone had opened a window. Long before the builders arrived for the day. Was someone sleeping, dossing, there? Who could it be?

For the next few days B kept an eye on the window but saw

nothing more. Maybe he had imagined it, but he couldn't help feeling excited at the idea of a secret neighbour. He felt an insane wish to push up the window and wave.

B had been born and brought up in suburban London – he was not by any stretch of the imagination a country lad – but he'd always been drawn to the natural world: watching birds and climbing trees whenever he had had the opportunity. His bit of London had been full of green spaces. And now, after some weeks of liberty, B began to hanker after a bit of green, a greater space in his outside view, some birds and beauty. He would not have known where to go outside the capital, and probably would have felt completely at sea. He remembered his one foray as a thirteen-year-old, when he had been on an exchange visit to a farm near Colchester. It was the first time he'd stayed away from home. He'd felt clumsy, ill at ease, completely ignorant of country ways, the machinery, where anything was, what anything was for, and he felt the family laughed at him. His opposite number, a stringy dark-haired lad called Tim, was used to milking, had even helped to deliver lambs, and had no time for a shy townie like B. But even in that horribly uneasy time, B had been fascinated by the difference in the way they lived. Tim had a level of independence that was outside B's experience, and he deeply envied it. Of course rural Suffolk was different from London, but it had its own dangers, as his parents had been at pains to point out. Nonetheless, Tim wandered freely round the farm without any constraint, as far as B could see. He wore the same dusty old trousers for the whole time that B was there, and B wasn't sure he washed. Tim certainly worked hard, but no one seemed to tell him what to do. Lucky blighter.

Most of all, B had been enchanted by the animals that he'd never seen up close: the soft eyes of the cows, the gambolling of the lambs. His delight had moved him out of his usual taciturnity, but his stumbling words were mocked by his hard-headed audience: *Aha, soon be on someone's table, that one.*

Despite his discomfort, that holiday had been a turning point. By the time he returned home, B was resolute. With nervous steps and tight fists, he approached his mother. The moment was vivid in his memory. She was doing the ironing, clad, as usual, in her National Trust apron, with which she covered her always-smart clothes when doing the household chores.

- *Mother?*

- *Mmm?*

- *I don't want to eat meat any more.*

She barely looked up. *Don't be silly.*

- *I'm not being silly. I don't want to go on eating dead animals.*

- *Well, you can think again. I'm not cooking different meals for you. As if I haven't got enough to do.*

- *You don't have to. I can just eat everything except the meat. There's plenty of protein in other things.*

She did stop then, put the iron down with some annoyance, and looked him in the face.

B, just stop this nonsense. You'll have the same meals as the rest of us, and be grateful.

And so began a war of attrition. B did not give in when he had made up his mind, and his mother, with acute frustration, knew that was so. She went on serving him meat, and he went on leaving it. But after a couple of months, there gradually appeared extra little things at meal times, such as nuts, and baked beans and eggs became more regular choices for tea. Not a word was said until Annette came home from uni and one day made a comment about only getting cheese on toast. Their mother mumbled something about "variety", and B was almost sorry for her, but he didn't help her out. His sister shot an eagle eye around the bent heads at the table and, for once, said nothing more.

Chapter 2

1997 was a momentous year. Yes, the world would remember it as the year that Princess Di died. And the year that Tony Blair came to power. For B, 1997 was the year that he left school. This milestone decision caused a terrific storm at home. For once, even his father chipped in. Having had to leave school at fifteen without qualifications – his parents needed him to earn some money – Dad felt strongly about education. B had stuck it out through GCSEs, had allowed himself to enter the sixth form – with Mr P's unexpected encouragement, he had even thought that "A" level art might be enjoyable – but halfway through the first term, he really couldn't hack it any more. He wanted out, he wanted his own life, not one dictated by his parents and teachers. Although he knew that without money that would be hard to achieve, he would not budge, and tried to think about what he might do.

That first term (he still thought of it like that) after leaving school was almost unendurable. He almost wished he had stayed at school: it would, at least, have kept him out of the house, where the pressure to find a job was almost as strong as it was at the job centre. He did a bit of dog walking for people who advertised in the local paper, which he enjoyed but paid peanuts: it was enough to supplement his pocket money, and not much more. The trouble was that any animal jobs either demanded qualifications that he didn't have, or were on farms, which he had no chance of getting, and after the ghastly experience in Suffolk, when his incompetence had been so painfully revealed, he didn't think he wanted. The London jobs were in pet shops or the zoo, and he couldn't stand the thought of seeing animals in cages all day.

1997 was also the year that Vicky was born. Annette, of course, made the most of the pregnancy and birth: feeling, though never it seemed actually being, sick throughout most of the nine months. Over supper every night B suffered a blow-by-blow account from their mother's daily phone conversations with her daughter. And every night he escaped to his room, punching pillows, almost bursting with the unexpressed shouting in his head.

It had been strange to see Annette in the last months of her pregnancy. Such a large bump on someone who prided herself on the slim contours of her body. But, to B's surprise, it didn't seem to faze her mainly, perhaps, because Rob was so obviously enthralled, not only with her for being so clever, but with the bump itself, which he stroked and patted with proprietorial pride. B couldn't bear to see it. His response took him by surprise. There was a fascination there, but it was mixed with a stronger feeling of – was it disgust? Yes, there was no other word for it. Maybe, it was because she was his sister, and any image of sexual relations was abhorrent. And maybe, he had to admit, there might be an element of envy of Rob. Insemination? For B? Fat chance.

The tension in the household built as the due date approached, so that even B felt an almost physical release when the news came that Vicky had finally emerged. When Mother left to spend a few weeks in Coventry to help Annette cope with the new baby, B relished the idea of spending some time alone with his father. But the time seemed to evaporate. His father was, of course, at work most of the day, and in the evenings Dad spent the time catching up on his paperwork, or on the phone making preparations for his next job. As B and his father sat down to the meals prepared and left by his mother in the freezer, they found it hard to talk. There was a giant-size hole in the household. Even in her absence, Mother dominated.

During the day, B walked a bit in the park, missing poor old Jeff more than ever. Walking just didn't have any point without a dog. He tried to get up early and run on a regular basis, but the momentum was lacking. He did go to the library from time to time, booking sessions on the computer, finding himself mostly among old men dozing in quiet corners, a few girls in headscarves and younger men engrossed in study. And of course he had to sign on.

The fortnightly trip to the dole office was an ordeal, queuing up with all the other no-hopers. It provoked one of the few outspoken criticisms from his father, who was a proud man, and had never signed on in his life. B had nothing against the idea of a job. He'd have liked something to occupy his time and take him out of the house. He'd have liked something to stimulate his mind, but had never found the right thing. The dole office were beginning to lose patience, suspicious that he wasn't really trying. He went to a few interviews, but never managed to find the answers that they seemed to want. He never felt that he made a connection or that they valued what he had to offer. He knew that people skills were not his strength. He'd have been content, for instance, with a backroom job in a library, but even that needed qualifications.

B was, of course, expected to attend the christening with his parents, and had to wear his hated and now redundant school blazer (he interpreted the insistence that he wear it as a pointed and deliberate punishment). They drove up the M1, turned into the M45, and went straight to the church. Apart from her wedding, he imagined it was the first time that Annette had entered a religious building since her days at Sunday School. He wasn't too keen on churches himself these days, and was even less so when he heard all the gobbledegook of the service – no wonder they had not asked him to be godfather. There was no way he could have said all that stuff.

He didn't even have the pleasure of listening to the beautiful old words from the Book of Common Prayer. Priding themselves on being modern parents, Annette and Rob had opted for an updated version.

- Do you reject the devil and all rebellion against God?
- I reject them.
- Do you renounce the deceit and corruption of evil?
- I renounce them.
- Do you repent of the sins that separate us from God and neighbour?
- I repent of them.

After the service, B got his first close-up glimpse of Vicky, and to his surprise, he was touched. She was so little. An uncle, fancy that! At one point, flustered by all the crying, and needing to go to the loo, Annette thrust Vicky into the nearest pair of arms, which happened to be B's. He was appalled at this flailing, screaming little bundle, and terrified that he might drop her or that her head would fall off. Then, all at once, the screaming stopped, B found his brown eyes fixed by two large blue ones – *I know you* – and his heart was won. He found himself enchanted by the little fingers exploring his collar, the warmth (and wetness?) of the little body against his. It was something completely outside his experience. Maybe, even at that early stage, he had recognised with considerable fellow-feeling, her awkwardness. *Stop pouring that bloody water over my head! Put me down, I don't want to be cuddled.*

As time went on, B could see that Vicky did not find favour with her mother. The dark-haired little girl was turning into a solemn anxious child, but one who – B was glad to see – was capable of sticking to her guns. When Ella arrived three years later, Vicky of course did not have a chance against the crowd-pulling little replica of their mother: pretty, winsome, and out for what she could get. Over the next couple of years, Vicky put on weight, and put herself at an even greater distance from the other women in the family, all of whom were not only blonde, but slender, in his sister's case to the point of obsession.

Vicky, he thought, would be about eighteen now. B wondered how she was faring. He didn't think her rebelliousness (if she'd managed to hang on to it) would have deterred her from going to uni. B rather regretted that his had. He'd missed out on a lot. But Vicky wasn't as isolated as he had been. For one thing, she got on well with her father. Whereas Annette had always seemed close to their mother – like as mother/daughter peas in a pod – and Ella had joined her in that triumvirate (or whatever the female equivalent was), Vicky was, as Annette put it, a "Daddy's girl". Father and daughter seemed to understand each other, and Annette didn't like it one bit. She, like Mother, did not hide her opinions or, in this case, her jealousy. Rob seemed a nice man. B would have liked to have known him better, but they lived far apart and were almost of different generations.

After a year or so of kicking his heels, B had a mini-breakthrough. Bernie Greaves, who ran the local corner shop (though it wasn't on a corner), had known him since he was a child and, taking pity on him, offered him a bit of part-time work. B loved the sense of independence that earning some money made, and getting out of the house, but it only lasted about eighteen months. Since B couldn't drive, and was unwilling to engage with the public, there was little that he could do. For a small shop, unpacking the supplies and price-stamping weren't enough to make him worth Bernie's while. But B was grateful for the short ray of possibility, and the bit of confidence it gave him.

What he wanted above all was to work with animals. He didn't have any of the right qualifications, or the sticking power to train as a vet, but it occurred to him that he might be able to help out. The man who had looked after Jeff all those years ago had seemed a nice enough bloke, and eventually B plucked up the courage to call round at the surgery. The same vet was still there but, no, B was told, he didn't need any help. However, a few months later he put B in touch with another vet, an Australian friend whose assistant had just left. B's history of cat-sitting and dog walking stood him in good stead, his five GCSEs were enough, and the job didn't demand any special qualifications. All the training, his boss, Laurie, told him, would be on the job. The pay wasn't much, and the hours could be very long, but looking after the animals was what B was after. As an urban practice, their staple fare was cats, dogs, hamsters and budgies, though there was the occasional more exotic pet, such as a young man who brought in a boa constrictor and an elderly woman with an equally elderly macaw.

The surgery was in Laurie's house, and there were just the three of them: the vet himself, B and the receptionist, Jenny, a stuck-up toothy girl with whom B had as little to do as possible. There was some tension about who did certain things, such as making tea or going out to buy biscuits. Jenny seemed to think herself too grand, and B certainly didn't think that was what he was there for. But he had to remind himself how much he needed and indeed loved the job, so he usually swallowed his pride. In any case, Laurie couldn't be doing with any hassle: he was too busy, and he made it plain that Jenny and B were dispensable – there were plenty of other people queuing up for their jobs.

B was given a loose blue outfit to wear. His uniform was known as scrubs: most appropriately, as scrubbing was mostly what he had to do. Scrubbing walls, instruments and cages, scrubbing muddy pawmarks off the floors and doing the laundry for the practice. He didn't let on to anyone about the nature of his work. As his family knew to their cost, cleaning was not exactly his favourite activity but, to his surprise, he didn't mind so much when it was for a job. He understood the importance of hygiene around sick animals, and actually took pride in the sparkling surfaces. There was a part of him that considered some of what he did as women's work, so he wasn't surprised to hear that male veterinary assistants were quite rare. But he came into his own when a big dog had been sedated and needed to be moved. Couldn't imagine a girl doing that.

His least favourite duty was labelling the bodies of animals which had been put down, before they were put in the freezer. He hadn't realised how much of a vet's job was ending animals' lives, and found that part of his job almost unendurable. Every time they were faced by a grief-stricken owner he was reminded of Jeff. Jenny called him sissy, and he thought her heartless. She was more at home with horses than with small animals, and B felt she didn't care. But Laurie made it clear that decisions were always made in the best interests, the least pain, for the animals concerned, and that was that. There was no room for squeamishness. B hadn't realised either how terrified nearly all animals were when they came into the surgery, in their cat basket or in their owner's arms: how they cowered and squealed, and were often violent in their need to escape. Touched by their fear, holding them with strong yet tender hands, B found he had a gift for calming them – a gift that even Laurie acknowledged.

On the whole B managed to avoid too much contact with the clients – that was Jenny's domain. But when she was on her day off or busy on the phone, he would be forced into conversation, although he managed to dodge too much of it by concentrating not on the owner, but on the pet.

Having a job gave some B some time to himself. Even during the hours when he was actually at the surgery, which could not be called free time, he was at least away from the house and the looming presence of Mother. For those precious hours his mind was his own. But the hours were so erratic that he could also extend his absence from time to time without arousing suspicion. He'd get brownie points at home while giving himself some blessed independence.

B loathed living at home. As it was, unattached, with boyish good looks, and still living with his mother, he was sometimes taken for a poof. But he absolutely wasn't, he detested the idea. It wasn't men but girls, women, who filled the fantasies of his night and day dreams. Over the years Mother had invited to supper one or two prim girls from church, with flat chests and straight mousy hair: when he could escape, B fled to his room –

these bore no relation to the heavy-thighed women that haunted him.

If he'd gone to uni, he'd have been gone long ago, but as it was he simply couldn't afford to leave. Only once he started working for Laurie was there a possibility. He tried to put up with Mother dropping hints. Didn't she realise that he was as keen to be gone as she was for him to leave? Despite his dislike of the telephone, he began to answer ads in the *Standard* for rooms in shared flats, but they'd always gone by the time he got through. He knew he was at a disadvantage by not being on email, but it happened so often that he sometimes wondered whether his way of speaking put them off or whether there'd ever been a vacancy in the first place.

In the end he was forced to rely on a contact of some church friend of his mother's, but it was bearable because she didn't know the people concerned, and the flat was a long way off. The East End wouldn't have been his first choice, but it was cheap and at a safe distance from the family home. They didn't know anyone living in that neck of the woods. Even if it meant travelling some way to work, the connections were good, and in any case it was worth it. Mother, in turn, was gratified that the contact had come from her and that, having a connection with the church, they were bound to be "nice boys".

But first he had to meet them. As he set off, a newly acquired A-Z in hand, and a couple of snaffled biscuits in his pocket, he felt this was a major journey in more than the literal sense, a feeling confirmed as, senses heightened, he emerged from the tube station to an unfamiliar but not unpleasant breath of exotic spice. Immediately outside the station was a bustling market: a row of stalls of heaped vegetables thronged around with black-robed women, and men with white caps and tunics over their trousers. This was uncharted territory, a different country. Mother would have had a fit.

At the little terraced house, a few minutes' walk away, he was greeted by a red door and, to its left, a black wheelie bin, spilling over with rubbish. Feeling nervous and unsure of what to expect, B paused for a moment before ringing the bell. When he did, a stocky young man with cropped dark hair opened the door, and smiled. *Hi, I'm Tony. And you must be B.*

Tony and his flat-mate, Malcolm, showed him round the two-up, two-down. He was to have the box room, on a lower rent than the others. That was just as well, as it was all he could afford, and he didn't need much room. The others made him welcome, but they didn't hit it off particularly and the "interview" was a mixed success. B was tongue-tied, but the others rightly sensed that he would keep himself to himself, and that suited them just fine. They both worked full-time, had active social lives, and wanted to relax when they came home. A deal was struck; B would move in the following week.

B had never had much stuff. Clothes didn't interest him, and he was always losing buttons, tearing his trousers on a rough chair, leaving scarves and sweaters on the tube. Mother had eventually lost patience with him and stopped insisting on fruitless trips to the London Transport lost property office. It was partly, perhaps, as a reaction to his parents' attitude to their possessions, but he had just never cared about "things". So a few boxes were enough to hold all he needed to bring.

The move felt momentous. This was at last the beginning of his independent adult life, and even his parents seemed pleased, offering advice and the cost of hiring a man with a van. On the doorstep with his belongings, B felt grown up. To his surprise, his mother leant forward and spontaneously pecked him on the cheek. It was a rare moment of affection and in that moment he hoped that one day, with distance, they might come to terms.

When it came to it, B realised he was scared. He remembered how disorientated he had been with those farm people in Suffolk. But that was as nothing compared to this. This time he had no home to go back to. He was on his own, in a strange place, with strange people – and a feeling of panic rose in his throat. Suddenly the confines of the parental home seemed unexpectedly comforting. Familiarity, however prickly and at times smothering, was still a blanket to be clung to.

The other two were astonished at how little he had brought with him. *Can we help you with the rest? What? Is that all?* Malcolm, the tall one, made him a cup of tea, and they left him to settle in. Settle in, and settle down. His new room was small but light, and he became calmer as he pottered about, sorting out his possessions: finding homes for his books, his notebooks and his clothes. The others cooked for him on his first night, and they sat down together and ate companionably enough. Tony was also a vegetarian: it was great not to feel the odd one out, for once. The others did most of the talking. They knew each other, after all, and B was content.

Looking after himself was quite an uphill struggle to begin with. Mother had always considered the kitchen her private preserve, so B had never really done any cooking. To begin with, he bought mostly ready-made meals, but eating like that was beyond his means, and after a while Tony took pity on him and initiated him into the mysteries of pulses, tofu and a wider range of veg. It was a revelation. Food at home had been pretty boring: an unwavering tradition of meat and two veg – only B didn't eat the meat. This was a completely different way of cooking, with Indian spices and vegetables available from the market and local shops that B had never seen before. The strange flavours took some getting used to, but it was wonderful to have so much choice.

But, after a few weeks, his contentment began to waver. His little tasters of other ways of living had been as nothing compared to the explosion of otherness that assailed him in the shared house. At his parents', no one seemed to care about who he was but came down heavily on what he did. Here, no one seemed to care, full stop. So, after being so used to battling against an imposed routine, a whole edifice of expectation, to have it suddenly whipped from under his feet, made him feel strangely bereft. His huge sense of liberation was accompanied by culture shock at the sight of trails of dirty washing, meals eaten at any old time, as often as not in front of the telly, or in bed, and people rolling out of bed at midday.

And one of those rolling out was a girl. When B took the room, he was under the impression that he was sharing with two young men. But, as often as not, there was a fourth member of the household: Malcolm's girlfriend, Bettina. B found it intolerable that she was there at weekends in her dressing gown; hugely put out that he could hear them banging away at night until he deafened the sound with a pillow over his head. He supposed she was trying to be friendly, but B didn't want to know. He'd had enough of living with women; she just crowded out the place and, besides, he was horribly embarrassed by her physical presence, especially when he knew she and Malcolm had been at it the night before. B wasn't used to seeing half-undressed women at the breakfast table and, to be frank, he was shocked. It offended his sensibilities. Some mornings he could almost smell the sex on her, and was so aroused that he didn't know where to put himself. What's more, he could see from her half-smile that she knew it. Fortunately he didn't have to see her, or his flatmates, that often. They were usually out in the evenings, and his own working hours were long and erratic.

Before long, the others made it clear that they were pretty fed up with him too. Tony was usually in a rush to get off to work.

- *Where's my milk?*

- *Oh, sorry, yes, I took some. Here it is.* B fetched it from the draining board. *I'd run out.*

- *Yes, and now you've left it out. For God's sake.* Tony took a sniff. *Pfah. It's gone off, you twat. Now I'll have to have my tea black. Last bloody straw.*

B found the "house rules" pretty incomprehensible. It all

seemed so petty. Malcolm's comment: *You haven't got your mother to clean up after you here, you know* both enraged B, and struck home. He'd buy Tony some more milk, and yes, he'd clean the bath in a day or so. He cleaned all bloody day, as it was. He didn't need to be nagged to do it at home too. It was as if Mother had stowed away in his suitcase. But he hung on. Even though he found it hard to manage financially, he was determined to make it work. This was his passport to freedom. Having struggled to leave, he couldn't bear the thought of crawling back to his parents.

He did visit them from time to time, but only because he was worried about his father. Dad had carried on working past retirement age – they needed the money – but in the end he'd had to give up. His joints were really bad, and he just wasn't mobile enough any more. Central heating was a very physical job and over the years he'd become very strong, but the arthritis undermined both his stamina and his mobility.

Even when he'd lived under the same roof, B had seen his Dad shrink, and hated it. He hated seeing Dad's usually spare face puffed up with steroids, seeing him wince with pain, struggle even with opening a jar of jam. Dad had lived for his work, and his fishing, and although he did sometimes stagger down to the river, it was all so much effort that a lot of the pleasure had gone out of it. So he was at home, under Mother's feet, as she made clear, and B himself had been desperate to get out. He felt guilty at leaving Dad to her tender mercies, but he had married her, after all, and B had a right to his own life. Didn't he? If he'd stayed, he thought he might have ended up doing her some damage.

B didn't go to see them often. He knew it was cowardly, but he couldn't bear to see Dad in that diminished state. Each time he went, he was shocked at how quickly his father had deteriorated, becoming increasingly breathless, struggling even to get up the stairs. When he stopped work, the heart had gone out of him. B guessed they had left it too late – *mustn't grumble* – and that Dad had put up with too much for too long. By the time they'd sought medical help the disease had too great a hold. On the last couple of visits, his father had been in the same armchair in front of the television, a blanket over his knees, and a defeated look in his eyes. When B asked what was being done, Mother said shortly that he was on all the medication, that they were spending a fortune on taxis going to the hospital and, she indicated, if he hadn't smoked for all those years, he wouldn't be having a problem. B hated her.

He was in the shower when Malcolm took the call: *B, it's for you*. B wrapped himself in a towel and went downstairs to the phone. *B, it's Dad*. Annette could barely speak, and he didn't need to hear any more. The inflammation from the arthritis had spread, it seemed, to the lining of the lung. He had collapsed at home, and had died soon after arriving at the hospital. All too late. B put down the phone and stood there. He was not surprised but he was devastated. He had seen it coming, but he still felt as if the ground had been cut from under his feet. Who would protect him now? He went back upstairs slowly. His dad. His lovely dad. And they'd never had that conversation, the conversation he'd dreamed of all his life in which they talked of their love for each other, their understanding, all they had in common, how they'd never really needed to talk. They knew. But now he doubted his certainty. Did he really know? Had he imagined it? He knew how he felt, but what about Dad? And had Dad known how much he, B, loved him? It was too late now. He blamed his mother. She had stood in the way. She had silenced them both with her withering tongue. As had Annette, who never stopped talking.

Was he now supposed to be the man of the family? He felt anything but. And, anyway, what had been his father's role? Mother had, as they say, worn the trousers. Provider, rock? B almost laughed. No one considered him anything like that, no one would expect anything of him. He was useless. Best he kept out of the way. Malcolm and Tony were kind when he told them, but awkward. They didn't know him, and he had no way of making things between them easier. He had to mention it at work too, to get a couple of days off for the funeral and so on. Again they said nice things, but no one really cared. No one knew how he felt.

The funeral was a farce: Mother had organised a service in her church, of course: a building Dad had hardly ever entered in his life. He'd had no religious faith: the priest hadn't known him, and what he said was a load of irrelevant garbage. Nothing had anything to do with the Dad he had known. The children weren't there: Annette didn't think a funeral an appropriate place for them, so they'd been left with a neighbour for the day. So there was not even a glimpse of Vicky to mitigate the gloom. He wondered how she was, solemn little thing. Mother and Annette were in black: even in mourning, B saw that Annette had to dress herself in some poncey outfit to show herself off. She was staying with Mother to see her over the first few days. He had no doubt that she and Mother had talked for ages about what they would wear. And Mother's crocodile tears. He wanted to scream, shout, hit someone. Instead, in a dumb fury, he obediently stood up, sat down and opened his hymn book but did not say or sing a word. At the end, while everyone shook hands and admired the flowers – *In Loving Memory* – B slipped out of a side door into the rain. He went back to the shared house, changed into his tracksuit, slammed the door, and ran. He knew he'd pay for his behaviour, but for once he didn't care. He had to get away, to express his furious grief in a clean way, in the only way he knew. He ran in the rain for about two hours, along streets then through Victoria Park, running almost blindly, pounding thoughts from his head. Back at the house, breathless, soaked and mud-splattered, he climbed the stairs, tore off his clothes, and crawled into bed.

When he could see beyond his misery, B could glean some

pleasure from the fact that so many had turned out. The rest of the family, of course, a few old friends and neighbours, and a number of strangers that he supposed were colleagues and clients of his father's. It confirmed what he had always known: that his father was liked, was a good man, had had a life beyond the limitations of his marriage.

B had thought that the practicalities of living in the shared house would be easy. He was cushioned, it was true, by just giving Malcolm a cheque for the rent each month, but in order to pay his share of the bills – and he was quite prepared to pay – he was expected to look at them and join in conversations about their accuracy, and the need to cut down. This was a world to which he didn't want to belong. Why was living, which had such profound and interesting possibilities, so weighed down and hemmed in with pettifogging paper? And insurance! People were obsessed by it. Home insurance, life insurance. What a negative way to live your life. He had nothing worth insuring, even if he'd wanted to, and didn't want to live in an imagined future where bad things happened.

It had taken a long time for the long arm of bureaucracy to catch up with him. When he'd lived with his parents, he'd heard them complain about council tax, mortgage, electricity bills and tax returns, but they were books that happily remained closed to him. It was quite bad enough dealing with social security, and the odd bank statement.

Even at the corner shop, there had been no problems. Bernie couldn't be bothered to put him on the books, so it was cash in hand, which suited them both. Once B got a proper job, it all changed. Income tax and national insurance, once just words, became a tiresome reality – and the complications of his change in benefit status were a complete nightmare. The advisors didn't seem to understand what they were doing, so how was he supposed to? After a while he ignored any post that came to him

– he never got personal letters anyway – so he stuffed the unopened letters in his sock drawer and let them fester. It got even worse once the NHS got hold of him. Endless eye-glazing and mind-numbing missives to receive and sometimes to sign. He did so as if through a specs-free blur of boredom and confusion. He wanted out of a world in which these things mattered.

But in general he was beginning to live his life. It was a strange experience, being free to do what he liked, no longer having to make excuses for coming home late. Having nothing to react to took some adjustment. After a lifetime of resistance there was nothing to push against. He'd longed for this freedom for so long, and had imagined all sorts of wilder behaviour – clubbing, girls, coming in at all hours, the release of a loud and boisterous energy. But that was fantasy; this was him. Having been restrained for so long, he had no idea of how to break free. None of that stuff really attracted him, anyway, even if he'd known how to go about it. Besides, he had to get up in the morning to go to work.

His journey in to the surgery was a pleasure. He didn't use the tube but had discovered a route that, although it involved more walking, was infinitely preferable. Indeed, the overground, the DLR, was a revelation. High above the roads and houses, B stared out of the wide windows at warehouses, parks and the spires of distant churches. While others plugged their ears and tapped on their phones, B felt he was opening up to the landscape of a country he had not known was his. As he gazed out, he felt an almost tearful pride, a faint and unfamiliar sense of belonging.

It was during his time at the shared house that B became eligible to vote. It wasn't as exciting as in 1997, when Blair got in and his parents were at loggerheads, but just going down to the local primary school and casting his vote was a proud sign of his having come of age. He could make a difference. The others didn't see the point, and he was rather shocked. All right, the

1997 result hadn't made the impact that Dad and others had hoped for, but it was still important to register an opinion. Although Dad hadn't generally talked about politics (he probably knew that his views weren't generally shared), voting had been one of the few subjects about which he had expressed strong views. *People have died for this right,* he would say. And he would march Mother and a protesting Annette, when she was home, down the road to do their civic duty.

B's new freedom also brought an unexpected kind of change. With more time to think, he found himself wanting to explore a different dimension. It was one that had been in the background for as long he could remember, but it had needed space, breath, to take shape. Having discarded the monastic goal in his early twenties, B realised that Christianity was not, had never been, at the root of his desire. Indeed, his yearning was based not on belief, but on a way of life. One day, he dropped into a Buddhist meditation class on his way home from work, and found it to his liking. The practice itself was both soothing and energising and, importantly, there was no need to interact with the others. Like the others, he brought his own cushion, and sat in the hall facing the wall. After the class, he did not linger, but changed into his outdoor clothes, and scrambled up the basement stairs into the street.

As time went on, practice became more a part of his life. He built into his day at home a time for meditation and bought a little timer for the purpose, timing himself, self-consciously at first, then as a matter of course. He liked the fact that the timing was complete in itself, had no relation to other people's idea of time. Fifteen minutes, a quarter of an hour, a tiny part of the rotation of the earth, of the pattern of the planets and the stars, not a part of the ordinary and artificially imposed structure of weeks and months.

He began to read about Buddhism, borrowing books from the nearest library, even buying one from the local bookshop, hugging to himself this new perspective, a new awareness of the sacredness of all created life. His love of the natural world and his decision to became a vegetarian all those years ago made even more sense, and he began to take more care not to injure any creature, however small. But the most radical change that he sought to introduce into his life was the practice of mindfulness. It was not something that came naturally. At the centre of his discomfort from childhood had been his clumsy body, always in the way, banging into things. Now, with greater concentration on every moment, every movement, he found a new carefulness, a new awareness of the thingness of things. As an awkward, headstrong person, he had to work hard at it. He remembered a lesson some years ago. On a walk on Hampstead Heath, his attention had been on the cloud formations and not on where he was putting his feet. He tripped over a tree root and broke his dominant arm. For weeks he had had to take things slowly, carry one thing at a time, but he hadn't, it seemed, learnt enough. His parents had always taught him to care about other people, but there were all these other entities in the world to be careful of – a daunting matter when one thought of nuts and matchsticks and flies and even particles of dust, but he soon felt that what mattered was not so much what he was being careful of or for, but the instilling of carefulness, mindfulness, in himself. Living in the present, in full awareness.

B had had to get used to an indoors life. That was how most people lived, didn't they? Work and home, back and forth. Even running had to take a secondary place. The need to escape, though, had not disappeared: it had just gone inside. He recognised now that his need for freedom was of the mind and spirit. His meditation practice, a practice of withdrawal, helped. He now lived apart from his family, he was independent: he had his own space and, most of all, his mind was his own. He had to deal with the odd eruption of anger and frustration, but a good run usually brought him back to a sane place.

He realised that he was living not only an indoors life, but an interior one – and of a different sort from before. In the past, he had bottled himself up. It was an inside that was full – to bursting, sometimes. This new kind of interiority was not about fullness but emptiness, purification, letting go. It had a completely different quality. Instead of stuffing everything tightly in to a bulging private self, in his daily practice he was concentrating on breathing *out*. Breathing out all the frustrations, anger and painful feelings that he couldn't even identify. In those moments when he could believe that in the end none of it mattered, he felt a strange sense of expansiveness, of inner space. *Let go.*

Over the months B noticed how affected he'd become by outward events. It was as if by spending more and more time alone, withdrawn, all stimulus was magnified. He was more opened up, more vulnerable to any event, however small. His increased awareness meant that he had to diminish the amount of stimulation in his life. Otherwise, it was all just too overwhelming. And in any case, all that information battering him from every billboard, screen and airwave – what was it all for? He'd never paid much attention to the news, and now began to question the very concept. Who was to say what news was? So, he gave up newspapers and, without explaining why, stopped joining the others for the nine o'clock news. *You've got to know what's going on.* Why? What difference did it make? But, living in a city, you couldn't avoid it altogether: there were headlines on the radio every hour or more, posters where they sold the *Standard*. In the world, "news" stared you in the face, whether you wanted it or not.

The other thing that stared you in the face was sex. Girls, women – he'd never been much good at them. They scared him. Even at school they had seemed so confident, so quick, so scathing of anyone who seemed a little less than, and his sister's friends were the worst. When they found he would not be mothered, they turned to teasing, seeing how he flushed at their attention. The girl in the shop had teased him, too, squeezing up against him in the store cupboard, asking him to reach for things on the top shelves in order to comment on his physique. How he hated it, wished they would all leave him alone. The problem was that he was not only repelled; he was fascinated, too. Fascinated by their bodies: plump and skinny, short or long skirts or bum-kissing trousers, and he was appalled at the piercings of one or two of them in the street or on the tube, sometimes in the lip or, horror, on the tongue. Imagine kissing that! And yet, as he grew older, he yearned, yearned in his flesh for kissing at all, for relief, for the satisfaction of a soft body under his.

He could barely acknowledge it even to himself, but he yearned even more privately, more agonisingly, in his soul for a lady-love whom he could protect, a damsel to whom he could be forever true. The two yearnings seemed to bear no relation to each other: the one somehow ugly, shouting to him from every advertisement and couple in the street, implicit in the playground, tormenting him in his youth; the other wrapped in boyish imaginings of knights, fealty and derring-do conjured up by the pages of those books about the Knights of the Round Table. It was excruciating even to think about it, but the vision was potent, insistent: an expression somehow of his truer self, whatever that was, not that he or anyone else would understand.

Chapter 3

B finished putting the shopping away, and surveyed his little store cupboard with satisfaction: the serried ranks of packets and tins, carefully arranged, with little room to spare. What quantities he consumed! As he refreshed his supplies week after week, he thought of all that stuff going down his gullet. Like pouring it in, on and on, kilo after kilo of cereal, potatoes, rice. All disappearing down the drain of his alimentary canal, just to keep the body going.

He grinned. The groaning shelves reminded him of Gran whose food stocks would have seen her through a six-week siege. Habits from a war mentality, he supposed. When she died, he and Annette had been sent to clear the stuff out of the kitchen, and found that much of the food was years past its sell-by date. In his own case, he was well aware of the irony, the hypocrisy even, of his full store cupboard. Living in the present, was he? With no care for the morrow? But the problem was that in one key way he did care about the morrow. He cared about his solitude, his independence. If he was forced to call for assistance beyond the faithful Hamid, he would open himself to discovery and the carefully constructed edifice of his life would collapse. So, his stocks of long-life milk, his tins of beans and tomatoes, his bags of rice and pasta, formed the bastion of his independence, a barricade against the outside world.

He was sometimes scared of his reliance on Hamid: the only person in the world who knew that he was there. Not scared that Hamid might break his silence – as a refused asylum-seeker, he had too much to lose: discovery would be more perilous than for himself and, besides, his regular payments were what kept Hamid alive. No, he was scared that something might go wrong with their weekly arrangement – the envelope pinned to the door with money and shopping list, the sack of rubbish, the discreet knock on the door signalling Hamid's arrival and the envelope with receipt and change slipped back under the door. Hamid might get ill or get caught, and have no way of letting him know.

B didn't unpack when the groceries arrived. The deliveries were always late at night, so when the receipt appeared under the door, and he heard Hamid leave, B carried in the separately packed bags, put the frozen food in the freezer and the other perishables in the fridge, and left the rest till the morning.

The crucial thing was that the two men never met. B was serious about his life as a solitary. The door was never opened until well after Hamid's departure. He had almost forgotten what the other man looked like. They had met some years before in a local shop, Hamid cashing one of the food vouchers (now withdrawn) and B on his crutches. Hamid had helped him on with his rucksack, and they had got talking. A slim young man, he had fled from Eritrea, and was at that time awaiting a decision about leave to remain. B had seen the meeting as "meant": Hamid was the answer to his need – he wouldn't say prayers – but his yearning need.

So they kept in touch, awkwardly in B's case, as he was ill at ease in company. He wasn't used to talking about himself and there was in any case so much that he needed to keep secret. But he could listen, and Hamid was keen to talk – about his family and his country, both left behind, although he always hoped to return. He was a handsome, intelligent-looking man in perhaps his mid-twenties, with a flattish broad face and extraordinarily smooth light brown skin. His father had been a journalist, and in 2005 had disappeared. The family had never felt safe: they knew that anyone could be taken at any time, and when Hamid had been called up for national service, he knew he could no longer protect his family and that it was time to leave. Like B, he had a sister, but she was younger than him, closer in age, and close in other ways that B couldn't imagine. Zahra had apparently been about to go to university, but the family's involvement with the political struggle had prevented her leaving home. Hamid was close to tears when he spoke of her, and how he'd had to leave without saying goodbye.

B tried to imagine it. What would it have been like to have a sister like Zahra: loyal, admiring, loving? He visualised her gazing up at him with tears in her eyes, throwing her arms around his neck: *Don't go, B. I can't bear it. What will we do without you? No, that's not fair. You go. You find a wonderful new life. At least we'll know you're safe.*

Hamid and his friends had left in the middle of the night, and eventually found their way to friends in Saudi Arabia, from where Hamid had applied to come to Britain. He had been here for over two years by the time they met, and his English was good, spoken with a rolling "r". He spoke without bitterness about the toughness of living as a non-person in a country he had thought of as a sanctuary. Despite being a qualified engineer, as an asylum seeker he was forbidden to seek paid work, and was met by dirty looks and sometimes abuse from fellow-shoppers when he cashed his vouchers. B had never met anyone like Hamid – didn't really know anyone who was black – and had had no idea of the kind of life some people had to live in this, his own, country. Hamid was much better educated than him, and B felt humbled by his acceptance of what many would find intolerable. Hamid said most of the people he knew were in much the same boat, and they kept each other going.

B saw some of the others once. He and Hamid had usually met in a cafe, where B always paid for their drinks, but on one occasion, Hamid said that he had little time, and asked him to come to the drop-in centre that he went to every week. B would not be able to come in – the security was tight – but they could have a quick word outside. The centre was in a church in central London, and to begin with B wondered if he was in the right place, as he waited outside. But then groups of people began to leave the building: an assortment of ages and nationalities. He was surprised at how well dressed they were: indeed, he had felt that about Hamid in the first place. Despite the scruffy conditions in which he lived, he was always neatly turned out, his beard trimmed closely to his chin.

B had always been told that people trying to stay in Britain were down-and-out wasters, like the homeless. But these, they were people of whom Mother might almost approve. And they were talking together with animation. People for whom English was not the first language were using it to communicate with each other. Brought up with a rather rigid idea of national identity, B hadn't imagined people of such different backgrounds finding common cause, and found himself moved.

When Hamid's appeal was turned down, B knew that their need for each other was equal. Hamid would be in danger if he went home; he had to stay here, illegally now. It was a revelation to B, and his salvation, that it was possible just to disappear, to fall into the cracks of visible society. That was what both of them had to do now – disappear. It had been Hamid who had found this place. With his ghostly network of men and women who to all official intents and purposes did not exist, he was in a good position to hear any whisper about a building likely to be empty for some considerable time, one that had some of the necessary mod cons, or could be reconnected.

The room was cold, even in the morning when the storage heaters had done their stuff. Even with both sweaters and his scarf on it was hard to settle down to meditation. Again and again B had to acknowledge his wandering mind and start again. Eventually he had to move his chair from its accustomed place to a spot nearer the heater. He was unsettled; it was unsatisfactory. When he went to the front room for his morning "walk" the windows were misted up but, once he'd wiped the peep-hole area of the glass a little, he could make out muffled figures: people walking, heads down in freezing rain, struggling with umbrellas turned inside out by the wind.

When B first arrived, the nights were long. When he got up in the dark he had no idea whether it was "morning" or not. He could only go by an innate trust in the rhythms of his body, a feeling of having had enough sleep and the gentle sounds from outside. Sometimes he knew that he'd got it wrong, because the "day" seemed interminable. For all he knew, he was getting up at 3am and going to bed at 5pm. But it didn't matter, and very soon the question didn't even cross his mind. Generally speaking, light was day and dark was night.

He used artificial light very sparingly. He couldn't use it at all, of course, in the front room. The light would have glinted through even the grime of the windows. But he also wanted to surrender as much as possible to the realities of seasonal light. Separated as he was from the impact of most of the natural world, he wanted to make the most of what was available. He did use candles from time to time: a gentler light that impacted less on his body clock: the only clock that had a place in his new world.

B's morning routine was a slow one: initially with considerable effort, as an exercise in mindfulness, but now, increasingly inevitably because of the pain. It took time for his limbs to accept a standing posture. It took time, too, to do anything with only one hand available, because of the need for a crutch. With his mug of tea, he took out one of his familiar books, and found a passage to spend some time with. When the tea was finished, he set his timer on the table beside him, and settled into a meditative posture. Sadly, he could no longer sit on the ground but his chair was carefully placed and, as at the meditation hall, it faced the wall, so that even if he opened his eyes, he would not be visually distracted. He was glad that there was little to distract him anyway. There were no pictures on the walls, which were themselves of an indeterminate beige. A light enough colour, anonymous, like him. The mantelpiece and cupboard tops were bare of ornamentation; just a few of his precious books lay on the surfaces.

He always removed his glasses before closing his eyes for meditation. Before and after his practice, the blurring of his sight helped the transition between the outer and inner worlds. He even began to think of his defective vision as a blessing. In fact, when mornings were dark, he often meditated with his eyes open. He had discovered that the area of the room in which he had placed his chair was untouched by outside light, so that his open but unseeing eyes would be met by complete darkness. These were moments when the walls evaporated, and he had a sense of infinite space.

B no longer needed an object to meditate on, but with his eyes open or closed he focused on the space between his eyebrows, and tried to empty himself of all thought. He found that practice, if not making perfect, did over the years improve his attention. Stray thoughts and feelings troubled him less. In the early days, his frustration was hard to cope with: the more he tried to get rid of distractions, the stronger their hold. It had been good to read that some considered the continuing returning of attention a spiritual practice in its own right. When distractions came now, he knew that acknowledgement was crucial: *Stopping, stopping, stopping, hunger, hunger, hunger*, or *itch, itch, itch*, gently allowing them to pass before settling again. On good days, he entered a spacious realm that stayed with him. It was as if there was space at the back of his eyes, space within the cavity of his body, between his organs, in his joints, as if they could all expand with his joy, breathe along with him.

Only after these practices did he wash and dress, and make breakfast, and go for his morning "walk".

Soon after his arrival, he was shocked out of his morning meditation by the piercing sound of a buzzer. *Where, what was that? No one knows I'm here. How could they have found out? Who can it be?* As it rang again, B, shrunk back in his chair, saw that the answerphone that he'd imagined dead was lit up, and the distorted face of a man with some sort of an official cap – a meter man? – was on the little screen. Eventually it, and he, went away, but for a few days B had a lurking anxiety about someone coming back to find him out.

Despite reassurance, B had always had a sneaking fear that someone might be inhabiting another part of this vast building, someone who might become aware of his presence. His separateness was such a key factor in his emancipation: the presence of someone else, however remote, would dash all possibility of total relaxation. This abode, after all, had been a pretty random choice. Everything had been arranged in such a hurry – not the central concept of it, not the dream that had been with him for an age, but the reality of the location. Only when they heard on the grapevine that a building had not only become free, but was likely to be overlooked by the authorities, could the dream of his refuge take form. The previous owner had died abroad, apparently, and it had proved difficult to trace his heirs. With all the battles over ownership that Hamid had been careful to discover, no one would be able to live here legally, and any demolition mob would be a long time a-coming.

It was one of B's small mindful pleasures that the two tasks of making a cup of coffee and toasting some bread for his mid-morning snack took the same amount of time. Putting the bread under the grill, taking down a mug from the rack – the medium-sized one was best suited to this time of day – taking the jar of coffee from the cupboard, the milk from the fridge, spooning in the coffee, turning the toast, pouring the boiling water into the mug, then the milk, then replacing the milk in the fridge – and the toast was done. He felt a vague unease at breaking his rule of doing just one thing at a time in mindful concentration, but the two activities seemed to belong together, to be part of the same intricate dance.

Or rather the processes coincided, for actual time rarely

entered the equation. Apart from a timer for meditations (and that time was not connected to any notion of a twenty-four-hour existence; it was just a finite period to give discipline to his day), he had no clock. He'd always felt at odds with time. He was fast when others were slow, slow when expected to be fast. His priorities were different. He cared about different things. Sometimes he felt like a dog being dragged away by an impatient owner just when he had found his favourite sniffing post. Now he could sniff to his heart's content!

B was always careful now to clear away the detritus of one activity before starting another. It was not just a matter of space, nor reacting to the remnants of his old clumsiness, but an attempt to maintain a clarity of mind, focus his attention and intention.

B's evening meal was the highlight of his day, and needed to be given time. Sometimes when he was tired, or when his fresh supplies were coming to an end, he would make an all-in-one stew that would do him for a couple of days: hearty and undemanding. He even had in the little freezer compartment of his fridge some packets of soya and Quorn shapes to grill. But they were a last resort. Only meat-eaters considered that protein had to come in sausage- or schnitzel-shaped pieces. He insisted that Hamid shopped at the market each week; B's fruit and vegetables mattered to him. Much he ate raw, and he tried to savour the individuality of each. When his teeth broke the skin of a tomato or a blueberry, he revelled in the burst of flavour that hit his palate. How could he have been so unaware in the old days, as he crammed food unthinkingly into his maw? In general, now, he tried to cook individual ingredients separately, plainly, so that he could taste their discrete flavours. Tonight, for instance, there were some early (imported?) broad beans, which had such a short season, a mound of plain basmati rice with a knob of butter, and a salad of vine tomatoes. He made a great deal of the preparation too: he took his time. It was a fragrant meal, and he made the most of the scent of the tomatoes as he sliced them and of the beans as he shelled them, leaving some of the most tender in their pods.

When the food was ready, he spooned it into a bowl and, with a crutch in one hand and the bowl in the other, hobbled to the table. He leant the crutch on the table and placed the bowl reverently before him. He straightened his chair in front of it. He shut his eyes and breathed deeply, taking in the scent of the cooked food, giving out gratitude. The family routine of grace before meals had stayed with him, though he'd given it a different, silent, form. Sitting down, he put a little food on his fork, put it in his mouth and once again closed his eyes, feeling the taste, the contrast of the textures, moving the food around his mouth with his tongue with a sensual, almost sexual pleasure. How hard it had been to school himself to eat in this way. How astonished his parents would be if they could see him now! All those years of telling him to chew each mouthful thirty-two times. Why thirty-two? And a hundred for coconut? For Heaven's sake!

Even now he sometimes yearned to guzzle his food, to cram it in, slack-jawed, stuffing in more and more with the insatiable appetite of his youth. His sister had found his table manners disgusting: *Oh, for God's sake, B, keep your mouth shut. I can't bear to look.* Resisting her had been an expression of both his hunger and a wish to assert his male independence, and it also represented a kind of tit for tat. He found Annette's attitude to food extremely irritating. It was an obsession with her, or rather her weight was, which came to much the same thing. She was, he was sure, envious of his easy approach, that he could eat anything, and never put on a pound. She was forever dieting, forgoing certain foods and then craving them. Their mother, who had had similar problems in her youth, was sympathetic, and did not complain too much about the demands it made on her household management.

Even now, B did not confuse mindful eating with "good table manners". He considered concentrated appreciation of his food to be part of his spiritual practice: an expression of gratitude for the plants, animal products and human effort that had gone into what he was eating. Sometimes he ate with his hands – or rather, as he gathered was the Eastern habit, with his right hand, savouring the extended experience as he ceremoniously licked each finger in turn. When he opened a new pot of yoghurt, he took a childishly rebellious pleasure in licking the plastic lid clean. Only care for his beard stopped him licking his plate.

B shut the door between the rooms when he went to bed. It was silly, almost superstitious, he knew, but he had a need for little rituals to demarcate one part of his life from another, night from day, sleep and wakefulness. In general, despite the pain, he felt he got enough sleep. Just occasionally, the restlessness of his inactive limbs drove him to a fury of frustration. No point, no point. Sometimes it was his buzzing brain that kept him awake. The trouble was that there was nothing, day or night, to distract him from his thoughts. Once a thread wove its way into his mind, it was hard to cast it out. Only in a long session of meditation could he finally let it go.

In general, he was not nervous, barely aware of the vastness of the dark uninhabited space around him. He certainly wasn't afraid of burglars. Even if they could get in, they were hardly likely to target a couple of dingy rooms in a dilapidated old house. Just as well, because he wouldn't be able to do much about them. In his weakened and destabilised state, a mere touch would send him flying. In any case, what was there for them to take? The delight of having nothing was that there was nothing to lose. No need for security, less anxiety, more peace of mind. Just occasionally, and particularly in the early hours, fear overcame his trust.

One night he awoke with a start. Rustling: he was sure he had heard it. Could it have been rats? He had heard that in London no one is more than twelve feet away from them. Ugh! Now that would test his love for other creatures. Why was it such a primal fear? Like vultures. Why was it so much worse to feed on carrion than to kill to eat? Just social conditioning, he supposed. Rationalising did not stop the pumping of his heart, so he lay breathing out into the silence until the fear left him and he sank back into sleep.

B had always been good at closing doors on the past too: a defensive action that shut out what he didn't want to remember. But no sooner had he slammed the door shut with the finality of this retreat than it began to bulge, crack open, pushed, it would seem, by the pressure of suppressed memory. Despite his best efforts to live in the present, he was overwhelmed by his past. With few distractions to defend him, he had to give way. He thought a lot about his childhood. It was almost as if he were recapturing some of that old – or rather young – sense of self. Much of the time in between seemed to have passed in an unmemorable, unsatisfactory way. It was strange how little of those later years he remembered.

Except for the accident.

All the clichés were true: both that it happened so quickly, and that it happened in slow motion. One minute he was crossing the road, and the next he was lying on his back, a motorbike skewed across the road, the driver reeling unsteadily and cursing with concern. But at the same time B remembered falling – so slowly, with time to notice the plastic bottle in the gutter, the brightness of the moon above. Everyone moved in slow motion and the scream seemed to come from somewhere else. It was only when he tried to sit up, when he saw the red mess of his right leg, that the horror began, and he passed out.

I didn't have a chance. He just stepped out in front of me.

Had he? B couldn't remember. In his confusion, he thought it was quite possible. That's what he did, didn't he? His head was always in the clouds, he didn't look where he was going. Steve, the motorbike bloke, seemed nice enough. Didn't run off, seemed distraught at what had happened, and even came to visit him in hospital. His own injuries were slight: a bit of concussion and a swathe of cuts and bruises, but nothing that wouldn't mend. If it hadn't been Steve's fault, B couldn't bear the thought of him going to prison. As it was, he'd probably be banned from riding that thing for quite a while. Another life ruined.

Mother couldn't understand his attitude. She became shrill in her disbelief. *You've got to fight it. He could have killed you. Just look what he's done. He's ruined your life. Murderous things, motorbikes. You see why I've never let you have one* until a nurse was moved to intervene and insist on some rest. And there was the question of compensation. There was no way he'd be working any time soon, and if it was proved to be B's fault, he wouldn't get a bean.

The first weeks after the accident were lost in a fog of misery. The hospital and the dentist – for he had lost one of his teeth in the accident too. It was a prominent one, and he would need to wear a plate. At twenty-five he felt that his life, such as it was, was over. No one would want him now. In the years that followed, he had barely had a day without pain. Only when he was on morphine after an op was he in blessed relief. Otherwise, it was a constant pill-filled struggle. How many ops? Five or six, he thought. The exact details were lost in the years of drug- and pain-induced fuzziness. They'd thought the first op a success, and had discharged him with a plaster cast, until he returned months later complaining of persistent pain, and an odd feeling of movement in his shin. He had, they discovered, what they called a "non-union fracture": a break that wouldn't heal. Trust him. So he was hauled back for more treatment.

Even in hospital he got the feeling that Mother and Annette visited out of duty. They were worried, of course, but once again he was a nuisance, he had put them out. He could see that they thought it was his fault. He wished they would go away.

B was hugely embarrassed the first time one of the nurses

gave him a bedpan, tried to cover himself up, until she said with frankness, *Don't worry, luv, we've seen it all before.*

That was no consolation. He didn't care about the others. This was him!

Life on the ward was a world of its own, with its own routines. B got used to, and even found comfort in, the set times of meals and medicines, of visiting times and rest. In a way, the rhythm was familiar. Mother's meal times had also been sacrosanct. Woe betide you if you were late. In fact, when he came to think of it, the whole of life in the outside world was dictated by clocks and bells. An alarm to get up in the morning, bells at school to indicate the end of one lesson or the start of break or lunch, clocking in and clocking out. He grew used too to the pills for pain, the pills to counteract the side-effects of the painkillers. The rhythm of pill, side-effect, pill, of exercises, rest, exercises, rest.

The inpatient and outpatient physios got to know him quite well in their tough but friendly fashion. When B was strong enough to take an interest in the outside world, he was amused at the shenanigans that went on among the staff. He had never watched a hospital drama, but began to understand the fascination. The hierarchies, the jostling for position, the flirtations no doubt, all taking place there in front of them all, at the central desk round which all the nurses, doctors, physios and OT people milled. Strange to see how some nurses slogged their guts out night and day, and others got away with skiving.

When B came round after the second op he was aware, through the blur of short-sightedness and drugs, of a pair of grave brown eyes gazing at him. Even when the inevitable nausea overtook him, the gaze stayed with him, and he fell in love. He knew it was a cliché, and it wasn't the nurse's uniform – he had heard enough playground smut to know that that turned some of the others on. It was her kindness. He had never known such a gentle touch, such a warm and, it seemed to him, intimate smile. Her name was Marion and, tucked tidily away, he could see a luxuriance of dark shiny hair. She asked him about his life, but there was little to say, and he was too tongue-tied to ask about hers. He was a little disenchanted when he saw her bestow the same largesse on the man in the bed opposite, but B was still drawn to her essential goodness. Such women existed: he had known it from his dreams but she was the first, except his gran, whom he'd met in real life.

He came out after the second op with plates and screws in his leg to keep the bone together. They'd thought it was a temporary measure at the time, and it did mean that he could put a little weight on his leg. The surgeon, Mr Rainer, was hopeful that this time, the leg would heal, and B would be able to go back to living a more normal life. The leg was a little shorter, but that didn't need to make much of a difference: they could give him an insole. But the pain didn't go away.

In the years after the accident, B's world shut down. Gone were his chances of an independent life. His job was gone and, without an income, he had to give up his place in the shared house. Running, his passport to a saner world, was out of the question – he could barely walk. The walls closed in. His life revolved round hospital and his mother's house. Yes, he had had to go back to living at home – or rather, with Mother, for it was not somewhere he thought of as home. Of course he could go out into the garden, watch the birds and smell the flowers; that was some consolation. But after his brief burst of freedom he was once more a prisoner, and forced into the dependence of childhood. And how he resented it! Reliant on Mother financially, subject to her will in all the doings of his day. Back in his old room, he'd been pushed to the edge of violence by his mother's assumptions of the old obedient ways that he'd struggled so hard to leave behind. The fierceness of his resistance, the passion with which he later pursued his dream, had been fired by those years of purgatory. The closeness of the fires of hell had served to stiffen his resolve.

In general, B put up with whatever the doctors threw at him; they presumably knew what they were talking about – that was their job, after all. But as time went on, and they still didn't get it right, his confidence in the medics began to wane, and his rebellious self began to assert itself. The crunch came when the consultant recommended a bone graft. Using bits of his own bone seemed to make sense, though he shuddered at the amount of carving up that that might entail, but when they said it would be topped up with bits from other people – discarded bone from someone's hip replacement, for instance, or, for God's sake, from dead bodies – everything in him revolted. His whole life, it seemed to him, had been a struggle to keep his own identity, to keep himself apart, separate. What was proposed would be to actually put bits of other people in his body. Dead people! The ultimate intrusion. Heaven knew what impact that would have on him: the history, genes of the person subtly infiltrating his unique (even if unappreciated) self. It was like something out of science fiction, being taken over by an alien presence *from inside his own body*. A dead and discarded alien presence at that. No, this he would fight with all his strength.

The Olympics were on at the time. In the lounge and on other patients' personal sets, the relentless TV was always on. Repeated images of that joyous physicality, that healthy exuberance, was almost more than he could bear. Not that he'd ever harboured any professional ambitions, but to know that he would never again escape into his rhythmic world, cover the ground on reliable striding legs, was an agony. The Paralympics were almost worse, especially when Annette, with her usual tact, encouraged B to think positively about what he might achieve even now. He was not bloody disabled, for God's sake. And he was not going to be. Not.

As it was, he'd had enough of being wheeled around in his dressing gown like some old codger waiting to die. He saw them all congregating outside, puffing on their fags, attended by their anxious and devoted wives. But he was young! And couldn't even hide under the guise of some "hero" back from Afghanistan. Amputation. The ultimate nightmare. It was not something that he had ever been prepared to contemplate, but the unspoken possibility that they might cut off his leg had always hovered in the air. True to form, as he sat with her in the kitchen one day, it was Mother who brought up the subject. *Maybe, B,* she said airily, as she placed the tea strainer on her cup, *maybe the time has come to consider it.* B stared at her, put down his cup, reached for his crutches and, without a word, left the room. *I'll see you dead first.*

Slamming the door of his room, locking it, he threw himself on the bed, trembling with fearful resolution. He could not lie still, but kicked his good leg against the wall, thumping it in frustration. At last, his whole being called *enough.* No way. His legs, his running, he was not going to accept the end of all his ecstatic freedom. Admit defeat. He would heal, he would. He stayed in his room, and refused to talk to Mother or Annette. He would not allow them to take his leg away from him. How he wished there was someone on his side.

He must have dozed off. B jerked upright in his meditation chair, alert to a strange acrid smell. Had he left the cooker on? Grabbing his crutches, he limped into the kitchen. Everything was off. And in the front room there was nothing either. He never had lamps on in there, and hadn't lit a candle for a long time. A fire somewhere else in the building? The thought gave him goose bumps. No one lived there. (B squashed an insidious worm of doubt.) Could electrics burst into flame of their own accord? Fear mingled with the sharp rawness in his throat. There was no fire escape that he knew of. He was slow on his feet and, although he was only on the second floor, he'd be trapped.

But, moving towards the windows, it seemed more likely that the smell was coming from outside. He peered through his peep holes. There, sure enough, was a little thread of smoke issuing from a window in the building opposite. A little crowd clustered as the fire engine arrived and water hoses were aimed up at the fourth-floor windows. At least there was no one in the building. B caught the thought, remembering the flicker he had seen that night. Surely not. If there had been, whoever it was would have been long gone. But if no one lived there, how had the fire started? Perhaps a paint-stripping blowtorch had caught something. B turned from the windows, forced himself to think of ordinary things, and went back to his meditation chair. He re-set the timer, removed his glasses, and shut his eyes.

B had started playing the alphabet game as a way of getting to sleep; now it was part of his routine. He'd been taught it by an old boy who'd been in the next bed to him a few years ago. B never expected to talk to anyone in hospital but Mac had been persistent, stopping off on his way from the loo to check if B was OK. He obviously had a need to talk, and B was a captive, if unwilling, audience. Mac sat on the bed and told B about his missus, and how he missed her now she was gone. He said he had played the game with her in a ping pong kind of way, taking it in turns to say words until they ran out of ideas or got bored. But it was, he told B, just as good on your own, a good way to pass the time. Anyway, B was thankful for the idea of the game, and had refined it, trying to find a word of five syllables or more, then one of four, three, two, one. That in itself raised interesting questions. How many syllables in, for instance, companion – com-pan-i-on, or com-pan-yon? How interesting that quite and quiet, composed of the same letters, were one and, subtly, two syllables. In his version of the game linguistically connected words, such as visit and visitor, were not allowed.

When B played the game, he usually began by drawing the letter of the day, trying not lift his pen from the page before the letter was complete, elaborating it with whorls and loops. The pleasure in the visual aspect of letters was one of the few things that B had gained from school. Those ornamented letters that he'd seen in the British Library had stayed with him and, even if he couldn't replicate them in any way, he could make more of the letters than their bald crude basic shape. Once he had the letter on paper, he began to enter into the game proper and paid attention to the possibility of what the letter might stand for. He had always enjoyed exploring the shapes of letters, but now that was as nothing compared with the rhythm, the sound, the feel, of words in his throat and on his tongue. He longed to open his throat, to shout, to sing, never mind how tunelessly, in whatever way to reclaim a voice silenced by familial scorn and by the music teacher at school: *No, not you, B, you'll spoil it.* He began to whisper the words to himself, rolling them sensuously round his tongue.

B had a curious relationship with language. He'd always been an avid reader. As a small child his keenness was a cause for congratulation, but the praise soon transmuted into criticism: *You've always got your head in a book. You never do anything.*

- *If B spent less time reading novels and more attending to his studies, he would do better in history/geography/maths.*

Even English lessons passed him by. Words, language: he loved playing with them but that wasn't what they did in class. Set books, essays, yuk! He didn't want to be told what books to read, or to pick them to pieces, he just wanted to succumb to their created worlds, to lose himself in other lives. For books gave him the exit from reality that he yearned for, and an entrée into wonder. He had always felt in his bones that life could be richer than the one he was living, and here was the evidence.

Surprisingly, maybe, he hadn't learn to speak until he was two, which was a source of frustration to his expectant parents but, when he did, it was in complete sentences. He began with, and had retained into adulthood, a halting and precise way of speaking, as if he lacked practice, and even in his twenties he sometimes mispronounced words that he had read and not heard spoken. He had remained a reluctant speaker. Not speaking in childhood was not a deliberate protest, though he knew Mother found it so. *You're just like your father.* It stemmed from his early difficulties with the physical obstacles of speech, and remained partly out of habit, and partly because he found when he did speak that the response both at home and at school was nearly always negative. Ironically, the one person with whom he would have felt safe to express himself was his father, but somehow the time was never right and in any case B was unwilling to break his father's obvious preference for a companionable silence, so he confined his confidential chats to the dog, and that only when no one else was around. It was strange that solitude should have loosened his vocal cords now, now that no one expected him to talk. Now that there was no one to hear him, he felt an overpowering need to express himself.

It was as if all the language he'd absorbed over the years was bursting out of him. Language that had been for his own delectation was now reaching out to an absent, or at least invisible, audience. Writing in his journal became a passion, his need for communication spilling out each night on to page after page. There was quite a little collection of journal notebooks by now, none of them as handsome as the first one, which he had chosen specially, but Hamid couldn't be expected to trail round town finding exactly the sort of book he liked, so B put up with it. As long as they were about the right size, had hard covers and the paper was plain, they would do. B wrote almost every day, but of course could not date his entries, and was careful not to count them to get an idea of how long he had been there. He just drew a little line under the day's entry to demarcate one day from another, and if he knew it, he also drew a little picture of the phase of the moon. Even in light-polluted London the moon could hold her own, as could Venus and, sometimes, on a winter's night, out the back in that enclosed dark space, he could see Orion too.

Words had always captivated him – the vastness of vocabulary, the infinite flexibility of their connections. An Oxford dictionary (sadly, only the concise one) had come with him as one of his precious collection of books. Today's letter was p, and he puffed the words out: "pon-ti-fi-cat-ing", "phil-an-thro-py", "pass-ion-ate", "port-ly". Nice word, that, and the letter p itself seemed to be portly, carrying its belly before it – and "pink".

An immediate image of Annette and her daughters rose up in his mind. Always in pink: pink dolls, prams, pink dresses. How did Rob stand it, going out with that trio of candy floss? If they'd had a dog, no doubt it would have been a poodle bitch with a pink coat. Pink. In the pink. What had pink got to do with anything, anyway? A colour's a colour, and it had always been line that had drawn him, that he had drawn. Not colour. It wasn't that he was colour-blind, just that he seemed unable to portray what he saw. Colour was in the eye of the beholder: pink elephants, Pink Panther. Peter Piper picked a peck – no, that's pickled, not pink. God, his brain was running away with him, giddy with the words. Almost like being drunk, he imagined, though that was a state he'd hardly ever experienced. Perhaps by now the women had matured from pink to crimson, fuchsia (fuck-sia), scarlet. Scarlet woman – that was a laugh. The epitome of a devoted wife, that was Annette. Not that he despised devotion. On the contrary. It was just that she was so smug. He could not imagine that in that ideal 2+2 marriage there was nothing hidden.

He could see her now, frozen for ever in that interminable series of photos that Rob had put up on his computer, and then insisted on showing them all. God, what a lot the digital camera had to answer for! Basking in motherhood, her arms protectively round Ella and Vicky, a self-satisfied smirk, and her little belly that boasted her maturity to the world. *See, I'm grown up now, I've been through the trauma and pain of childbirth, have grown out of all*

those silly fixations about my weight. I know what it's all about now.
So this is what all those girlish giggles and crushes had led to.
She had got her man, and now delighted in her new kitchen, her
plasma screen, their little bungalow on the outskirts of Coventry.
So much for her boasted college education. He remembered her
saying that she would go back to work once Ella was at school.
Maybe she meant when Ella finished school. Not that their
parents had ever criticised. She was the golden girl, after all, and
had produced grandchildren. There was no answer to that. No
wonder Rob looked care-worn. Keeping up with the demands of
his womenfolk took some doing.

He wondered how Vicky felt about all that pink: he didn't
think she was a pink sort of girl. She didn't look away from the
camera the way he had done as a child, but she didn't smile
either. He hoped she had managed to keep her spirited independence. **V.** V for Vicky. V for victory – he hoped so.

He'd always been called B, and had never really known why.
Maybe it was because neither his father nor Mother liked his
given name, that it had been a compromise when they failed to
agree, or maybe they thought it didn't suit him when he
appeared. And it was B not Bee – Annette and Bee, could almost
be Ant and Bee, those books he'd liked so much as a child,
though he hardly identified with the horribly sensible Bee.
Anyway, Annette was A, he was B, and that reflected their status.
If there had been a third child, would he or she have been C? But
as he explored the pictorial possibilities of the letters, he was
again drawn, as he had been in those manuscripts, to the letter B.
He liked the shape. It had to be the capital: symmetrical, double,
the shape of a Gemini, like him. In his journal he doodled letters,
especially the letter of the day, but also, again and again, increasingly elaborate versions of the letter B. His letter. And he
reminded himself that B stood not only for second-best but also
for Brave, Bold and Beautiful.

Chapter 4

His mother's death changed everything.

B was back in hospital at the time. She was alone, and had just collapsed on the kitchen floor. When Annette got no answer to her nightly phone call for two evenings in a row, she'd sounded the alarm, and the police had broken in and found Mother dead. Apparently she'd had a heart condition, and, according to the family GP, she could have gone at any time. Of course B was sad, sorry. He grieved – he had a lot to thank the old…woman for, but he was not broken-hearted. She'd never understood him, never seemed even to love him, and it was hard to understand her constant disapproval, not only of him and his father, but of much that he felt mattered. Living with her had been too much like a boot camp.

The doctors reluctantly allowed him out for the funeral. He'd had a new contraption fitted, and they wanted him to have another couple of days to get used to it. It was a cumbersome circular sort of leg brace with pins attaching it to his leg: pins, he understood, that went right through to the bone. By some marvel of physics which he had yet to understand, the external rings and rods created a tension that relieved the broken bone of pressure while allowing healing to take place. It also allowed him to put weight on his leg without pain.

As he got out of the taxi, B felt wobbly and strangely distanced, as if he were seeing the parental home for the first time: a pokey little place, with neatly tied back curtains, bars on the ground-floor windows and a freshly painted peach front door. As he and his crutches limped up the path, he felt the familiar sinking of his stomach and, letting himself in, half-expected Mother's rasping voice to call to him from the kitchen. It was very odd to be in the house now that she'd gone, but he didn't feel she was entirely absent. Something like a shadow lurked. The house was still thick with her presence. But his mood lifted at the sight of Vicky in the sitting room, although he was surprised to see her lying with her feet up on the impeccable cream-coloured settee.

- *Hi Vicky*, he said. *You OK?*

- *Yes, thanks, Uncle.* Uncle, that was nice. *Just a bit of a headache, and, anyway, I like lying on the settee.* They grinned at each other. Both knew that in Mother's day, it would never have been allowed. A sea-change. And Vicky was the first to mark it.

- *That's my girl*, B thought, but did not say it.

Vicky was now in her teens and, as he'd expected, she had grown into a sturdy young woman, with strong eyebrows, long dark hair, and a reticence that reminded him of himself. But, unlike him, she enjoyed school, and when he asked about it, she came alive. Some of her teachers, she said, were *really cool*, and were encouraging her to go on to study languages, though she hadn't quite chosen which A levels to do. Strong minded and level headed. He was so glad that life felt good to her, and that there was one female member of the family whom he could actually like. It gave him hope. Ella, on the other hand, pretty as a picture, if you like that kind of thing, was ever the young madam, tossing her head with a decided air, whenever she had something to complain about. How strange that two girls, just two years apart, could be so different: one dark, one fair; one self-contained, the other self-centred. Just like her mum.

At Annette's request, the undertakers had left the coffin open for a few days. B was flabbergasted. Where did she get that from? One of her trendy magazines, perhaps. But, anyway, at her insistence, B went with an ill will to pay his respects. On entering the room where the body lay, he reluctantly walked over to the coffin, and, with a sideways look, glanced down. He felt an unexpected pang. It was the first time he'd seen the face of a dead human being, and it didn't look like the mother he knew: it was a serene and, yes, a pretty face. Was this the face that had so captivated his father? What had gone wrong in the intervening years? The lines were sort of ironed out: all resentment and disapproval melted from it, gone. Like the spirit, they had obviously left the body. Was it part of spirit? Part of something that lived on somewhere in the universe? Perish the thought. He hated the thought of all that negativity swimming around.

Annette and the girls stayed on at the house after the funeral. It was just as well; B was still pretty shaky and would have found it hard to cope on his own. He generally kept to his own room. It was his refuge: messy, as he'd left it, with its own familiar and comforting smell. He didn't venture out much, except for meals and, remembering Annette's habitual nosiness, he was careful to lock the door when he left. He skirted Mother's room with unease: there was no way he would go in there. Annette seemed to have no such qualms and roamed freely around the house, calling out to her daughters, and exclaiming at this and that. B had the distinct impression that his sister was casting her eye over the possessions she hoped to make her own, and totting up the possible value of those she'd want to sell. She was even taking notes. B didn't much care for himself – there was nothing he would want – but he disliked the ugliness of her greed.

The three women spent a good deal of time sorting through Mother's clothes and so on, but one day Annette asked B if he'd come and give her a hand. He felt a distaste. Why would he want to go through all that stuff? Especially stuff that Mother would never have let him touch while she was alive. But apparently it was with the photos that Annette wanted help. That made sense: the girls, after all, would have no memory of what the earlier ones represented, so after lunch one day he joined Annette in the sitting room. B absolutely didn't want the photos – thank God Annette did – but, as they sat side by side on the big settee, and opened up the albums, some of the pictures caught his attention.

In the early photos, from before he was born, he could see, in his mother's classically beautiful face, the beginnings of those familiar lines of dissatisfaction. By the time B had been old enough to notice it, the fine red mane of her youth had faded and was interspersed with grey. For his father, she had always been the beautiful young woman of whom he had been in awe. Dad had never quite believed that she could think highly enough of him to marry him and, in later years, despite the fact that her tone to him was often infused with contempt, he would never hear a word against her. He treated her with old-world courtesy, always handing her on and off the bus, in and out of the car, ushering her first through the door, even when she was perfectly fit, and he himself was becoming frail. He simply could not do otherwise.

Until Rob appeared on the scene, Dad was the photographer of the family, so he often didn't appear in the family groups, but when he did, he was always sitting close to her, with eyes only for his lovely wife, not for the camera. Dissatisfaction and adoration: B could see that they were both present in the marriage from very early on.

There was lovely little Gran, sitting upright at the front, with her tight little white curls, and her bag in her lap. And there behind her, one hand resting on the back of her chair, was Granddad, with his broad face and almost equally broad smile, standing sturdily, face-on to the camera. From all accounts he'd been a larger-than-life man: the life and soul of the party. He had died a few weeks before B's birth, and the two events were forever entwined in his and, he thought, his mother's mind. He had always felt that it accounted for Mother's attitude to her son: that she couldn't think of him without thinking that he had somehow taken her father's place. B wished he'd known his grandfather, although he also felt a sort of resentment about the man whose death had eclipsed his arrival.

But later he came to realise that he'd got it wrong. Actually Mother didn't really like men at all; her dislike for B had nothing to do with the timing of his birth, but was only part of a general attitude to the whole of his sex. Look at how dismissive she was about Dad, and how she referred to couples only by the name of the wife. What was that about? Maybe Granddad hadn't been the ideal father after all. There was no way of finding out now, and anyway, B was more concerned about his own life in the present, and in a possible future too.

As Annette turned the pages of the album, it was interesting to see how, up to the age of about four or so, he himself was smiling, however insincerely, and that after that the smile had faded from his face. To start with, he imagined, he'd been eager to please, and then it was as if he knew he didn't please, so there was no point in making the effort. B was rather taken aback to realise that he'd understood so much so early, but then his mother hadn't made much effort to hide her aversion, and his father, in his silence, did nothing to counter it.

B had come to admire that silence, that air of self-containment. In fact, he liked to think that he'd taken on something of that same quality himself. In his present way of life, of course, there was no alternative, but he'd made the choice in the first place and was simply living it out, that chosen life of silence. He didn't know if his father's motivation had been spiritual, knew next to nothing of his father's motivations. They had just never talked. And he regretted it now. Beyond the fishing, beyond the idolisation of the women in his life, there might have been something, something in the silence which united them. Sometimes he had caught a steady look from his father which he felt indicated understanding. He liked to think so, though he couldn't be sure what that look signified. By the time B had hobbled out of the hospital that last time, his father had been long gone, but he liked to think that his father would have been with him in that decision, would have spoken up, have helped B in his fights against the medics, and against his sister.

After Mother's death, Annette took a commanding role as older sister. She had always had a tendency to be bossy, but now, as the oldest in the family, she became insufferably overbearing. She was adamant that for B the operation was the only way forward, impatient with what she regarded as her brother's obstinacy (*typical*), and high-handed in making plans for his, B's, life. *You will of course have to come and live with us. You obviously won't be able to cope on your own. Once the money comes through from the house, we'll be able to get something bigger, and fit you in.* B felt rise in him his inner growl. They were writing him off again.

In the event it was a year or two later that the matter came to a head. Had it been Annette's influence? He would never know. B was in hospital again, for yet more tests, and one morning, during the ward round, with a couple of junior doctors in tow, the consultant addressed him with a grave face.

Mr - , over the years, as you know, we have tried our best to save your leg, As you won't accept a bone graft, and in any case, I think we might be beyond the usefulness of that procedure now, I fear we have come to the end of the road.

B stared at him, stared at his stuck-on gravity and shiny pointy shoes. *End of the road, maybe,* he thought. *But what's this "we" business? It's just for me, mate, not for you.* But, yes, he supposed it was the end, and with that realisation came a sense of release. Hope was very tiring, and it would be a relief to let go. *Yes,* he said out loud, *I suppose it is.* But in B's mind it was the end of a very different road from the one that Rainer had in mind.

So, the consultant was continuing, *I fear our only option is to amputate. We'll obviously keep as much of the leg as we can, and there are excellent prostheses available these days. After years of pain, people often find it a relief, and you'll be able to go back to work, live a normal life again.*

As Rainer spoke, B felt in his gut an up-welling of fury, a volcanic resistance to all the happenings of his life, in which it seemed to him that he had had no say. The powerlessness of his youth, the accident, the years of pain expressed in a body, which now they wanted to take over too. *No,* said his body from his gut. And then from his vocal cords: *No.*

The consultant paused, and the pens of the junior doctors hovered over their notebooks.

- *What do you mean, no?*

- *I mean no, I won't have an amputation.*

- *Please, Mr - , I quite understand your distress. But this is a big decision, please take some time to think about it, and have a chat with your family.*

B consented, knowing that pretending to have those discussions would buy him valuable time. It helped that the conversation took place on a Friday. Everything ground to a halt over the weekends, with no doctors, no physios, only a skeleton staff of nurses looking after the patients and running the basic services. But there was nothing to think about; the decision had been made before he'd come in. In fact the idea had been with him for years.

From the moment he began to recover from the devastating effects of the accident, B was aware of a very odd conviction creeping into his consciousness. What if the accident that had smashed his previous way of life was some sort of a blessing? Maybe out of that destruction something else could grow. Something that had more life than the miserable existence he had been clinging to all these years. Once he came to terms with the fact that it was unlikely that he would ever completely recover the use of his leg, B began to wake up to the hidden grace of that limitation. Only out of this devastation, it seemed, would he find a way to fulfil his soul's desire. Utter solitude, separation from the world. An astonishing thought, but for some reason it seemed to draw him like nothing else. He'd thought about it for as long as he could remember, and now that he was faced with the possibility of putting his dream into reality, there was no fear, only an intense excitement. The difficulties lay in fobbing off the intrusive, if well-meaning, efforts of family and the NHS, and sorting out the practicalities of living.

A month or two before he went into hospital that last time, B rang Hamid and arranged to meet in their usual cafe, after the lunchtime crowds had left. The Italian waiter knew them by now, and greeted them with a friendly smile as he went to clear the dishes off their favourite corner table. As usual, Hamid did most of the talking. Despite the fact that English was not his first language, he was a more fluent speaker than B, and seemed sensitive to B's vocal inhibitions. Once B had haltingly described his idea, Hamid got the point immediately and ran with it, began to plan all the research he would need to do, even to make preparations. B was scared, felt that it was all running away with him.

There's one thing I don't understand, though, said Hamid, as they took off their coats and settled down.

- *What?*

- *Why you want to be on your own. Why you don't even want to see anyone. Won't you be horribly lonely?*

How to explain the depth of his need? For escape. His yearning to leave behind his life-long discomfort with other people. How could he explain that being alone was all that he craved. How to describe the postcard picture of the hermit that haunted him like a part of his essential self. He had never spoken of such things. He knew it would sound silly, and he dared not risk exposing himself to ridicule. It was too precious, too close to his closed-in heart.

Hamid saw his discomfort, and didn't pursue it. It was B's business. He changed the subject to more practical matters. *You know it's illegal now.*

- *What?*

- *Squatting.*

The word jolted B. He had assumed that squatting had always been illegal. It was one of those activities associated with other people, the sort his sort were never likely to meet. Was that what he was contemplating doing, *squatting*? The word conjured up an image of unkempt down and outs barricaded into other people's (*proper people's*) houses. Such ugliness bore no relation to the glory of his vision, the beauty of what he was planning to do. He saw that Hamid was looking at him, and realised that he knew what was going through B's mind, had wanted to shock him. For Hamid and his friends, of course, whose whole existence in this country was outside the law, another illegal act would make no difference. But for B...becoming an outlaw meant changing his whole view of himself.

He tussled with his discomfort. He'd always been a law-abiding bloke. True, he had never felt part of society, part of the world that his mother and sister seemed to inhabit with such ease, but did that mean becoming more at home with the people they had always despised? And it seemed wrong, thieving, really, to fiddle the electricity. If he could have paid someone without them interfering in his life, he would have done so, it was only fair. But his life depended on anonymity, so something had to go. He was doing what he was doing because he had to, because it was the right thing to do. He'd fought so long for his chance. He couldn't allow other people to destroy it.

B knew that some prisoners held in solitary confinement went to extraordinary lengths to mark the passing of the days, scratching the walls as if their sanity depended on somehow keeping tabs on the world of time. In his self-imposed solitude, B had no such need. Quite the contrary: it was with the greatest reluctance that he allowed any awareness of time to enter his life at all. The only kind of timing that he was forced to observe was to count the days so that he didn't miss Hamid's visits. If he did, there would be no order for the following week, and he wouldn't know when to wait for the gentle knock on the door. Since Hamid always called at night, when he was due B had to force himself to stay up. On the one occasion that he'd forgotten, he'd been alerted to the presence of the groceries only in the morning when a puddle had formed under the door from the defrosted frozen food.

So, B knew about each of the weeks as they passed – he just didn't know how many of them there had been. Indeed, he went to considerable trouble to avoid any such knowledge. He was careful not to count his diary entries or the slowly diminishing stack of bank notes under his mattress. He did not want either to mark the weeks that had gone, or anticipate how many more he could fund. It would be enough. All would be well.

Sometimes, even without a clock or radio, he had more awareness of time than he wanted. He didn't know when the heaters were programmed for, but knew evening was not yet upon him until he felt the heat rise into the air. Early evening was always when he needed his thickest sweaters; on the coldest days he even reached for his sleeping bag. The days were still short. Hibernation time. Had Christmas come and gone? No sweat if it had. What a relief to avoid all those hyped and extravagant expectations. He shuddered to remember the Christmas lunches of his childhood with Annette and Mother talking to each other as if no one else existed. No different from any other meal except that the rest of the family ate turkey, and they all wore paper crowns. Annette fussed about the colour of hers; Mother was careful to perch hers in a way that would not disturb her coiffure. And there was the stronger than usual guilt-tripping over his need for a different meal. Every year he wondered, with increasing dread as the date approached, how he was going to endure it. Even when he'd moved out, he didn't have the courage to stay away. The others in the house went to their families for Christmas; it was what people did.

And as for presents! He had no idea of what to give anyone, and resented spending money on pointless things. The others probably felt much the same. All those false smiles and thanks for more and more useless objects. In a fit of generosity one Christmas, Annette had given him a mobile phone. She had shown him how to use it, and put her number on it, and B had added Dad's. Even if he never used it, it gave him some sense of comfort to know that he could get in touch with Dad when he was away on a job; it lessened the distance between them. But, otherwise, whom would he call? The phone sat in the drawer with his socks. Annette, of course, couldn't imagine anyone being without all the latest gadgets. He expected that she and the girls had everything that was going: the iPod, iPad, blackberry, raspberry, whatever. Rob would need a phone, of course, but B couldn't imagine him with all the rest of the paraphernalia: he was much too sensible.

And were they now in a new year? He had no idea. All he knew was that his new year would start when the days got longer. More light, new life.

In the outside world, time was of the essence, and there was no getting away from it. Even in the street below, life was marked out by little parcels of time. He began to get used to the local rhythm of human activity: the twice-daily routine of the refuse lorry, with its lights flashing in the dark; and for past months the activities of the workmen at the house on the right. He knew it was after 7.30 in the morning when there was a little collection of men in hoodies standing around outside, stamping their feet.

He didn't worry about being seen. Even if the dark and smeary windows hadn't blanked him out, he knew that no one would be looking. No one looks up in cities. And no one expected him to be looking down. He supposed that by now he had a distorted view of reality – the figures immediately beneath him were foreshortened, although he imagined that people in the distance were reasonably in proportion. He found it interesting that despite people's habitual self-consciousness the passers by never imagined that they might be spied on from above.

When there was little to interest him in the street, B looked up instead. He looked again and again at that window opposite, but had never seen another flicker. Whoever it was must have gone.

He had a fellow feeling for whoever it might have been that was hiding out. From what Hamid had told him, B could imagine that there were, all over London, all over the country in fact, thousands of unknown lives. A hidden population. Maybe these were his people, people who would understand.

These rooms weren't that high up but even living on the second floor brought him closer to the sky, and facing an open street gave him a wide vista into which, even from behind closed and blackened glass, he could breathe. On good days it raised his perspective from the nitty gritty life of the little people below, and drew him to the sun, the sky, and some intimation of what lay beyond. And then there were the clouds. Although he had always been drawn to the sky, especially at night, B had never been so aware of clouds. Not on overcast days, when a pall of beige masked the heavens from his sight, not on the rare days of unbroken blue, but at other times through his peep holes he could view a patch of sky that was transformed from moment to moment as the heavens went on the move.

The sky was a continually changing canvas. Sometimes the movement was slow, as a cloud inched its way from left to right; sometimes it sailed with grandeur, sometimes it raced across his vision, as if pursued by a storm demon. He tried to focus on one cloud at a time as it passed in front of him, but it was hard to identify it as the same as it stretched, broke up and coalesced with another. Sometimes a whole body of cloud would float across the sky in an unchanging three-dimensional entirety. At other times the clouds were still. Grey, white or light-filled yellow; fluffy and ethereal, or a solid bank, low in the sky, impenetrable, and iron grey. In the evenings, occasionally B glimpsed a few little pink clouds to his left, a reflection, no doubt, of a sunset, unseen, blocked from view by the buildings on his right. The clouds became a constant source of fascination. He wasn't interested in sentimental interpretations of the shapes as rabbits or faces: a cloud was a cloud and in itself held endless possibilities.

Faced with the same view every day, he was aware, as he had never been before, of the transformative impact of weather. On an overcast day, he saw how the buildings were seeped of their colour and interest: dull buildings on a dull day. And how quickly on a bright day everything changed when the sun disappeared. And how his own mood was affected too. A dull man on a dull day. He didn't suffer from SAD, but he could see how people might. For him the outside mattered less than it did. He had his life inside.

Money made all the difference. In her dying, Mother had facilitated B's new life. In his recognition of that exchange, he felt something had been laid to rest. Maybe therein lay the seed of forgiveness.

There was little in her estate apart from the house. She'd left a chunk to the church and the rest (whatever her feelings, she was fair, he had to give her that) was divided equally between Annette and himself. Even after the mortgage was paid off, there would be a good bit left. When they learnt the terms of the will, Annette started to complain that B didn't need as much as they did. He had only to fend for himself; she had two children – but Rob, ashamed of her greed, soon shut her up.

Probate had been granted relatively painlessly. The estates Rob worked with, it turned out, were not those of landowners, but those left by people who had died. Although not a lawyer, Rob knew his way though the intricacies of this particular bureaucracy, and Annette implied that his knowledge had smoothed the way. Whatever the explanation, B was grateful. And Annette was cock-a-hoop. Although she obviously grieved at the loss of her mother, she was thrilled to have some real money to play with at last.

B wondered what to do with it all. He'd never had much money before, and what he had sat in a current account. There hadn't been enough to bother about, and even if there had been, he wouldn't have bothered. Suddenly there was a lot, and all the jokes about low interest, and "you might as well keep it under the mattress" seemed to make sense. It would be immediately accessible, he could keep tabs on what he had, and no one could snoop or track him down. There would be no information that he needed to give to anyone.

Closing his account at the bank had felt like an exciting first step. It hadn't been easy. It was a newish account and, as B got his money from a hole in the wall, the staff at the bank didn't know him. How amazed they must have been when all that money came flooding in! Despite phoning in advance to alert them to his intentions, there was surprise, maybe even suspicion, as B asked for the whole amount in fifties, which he put into the rucksack brought for the purpose, but he had all the necessary ID, and no one could stop him taking his own money.

Before he left for the hospital for what he knew would be the last time, in the room in the parental home which he inhabited between hospital stays, B packed a bag with everything he would need. Into it he put the large wad of bank notes in a paper bag tied up with string, his meditation timer, a few precious books, paper, a specially chosen notebook for his journal, pens and pencils, the jigsaws he'd bought, and the special kit, all his underwear and his specially adapted clothes, his other trainers and a pair of sandals. He was careful to pack the prescription for his specs – if anything happened to them he would be done for. He left behind his radio, his gum boots, and all the knick knacks of his life.

The binoculars posed a dilemma. With one of his first pay packets from the surgery he had treated himself to a natty little pair, and he was loath to give them up. Although, since losing Jeff all those years ago, he'd never been a great walker – why walk when you can run? – he'd recently taken greater pleasure in trips to the local park to watch the birds by day and the stars by night.

For both, the binoculars enhanced his pleasure. But now, for the interior life that he planned, what use would they be? Although it was hard to imagine his exact circumstances, B expected to be enclosed in some inner city space, and his attention would be within. So, he left them behind.

Being without music would not be a deprivation. His parents had quite a sophisticated hi-fi system, to which they often listened in the evenings, and Annette was usually plugged in to her mp3 player, but B couldn't bear the feel of anything stuffed into his ears and, it seemed, had missed out on the musical gene. Rhythm, yes: he loved to hear drums, for instance, but he simply couldn't recognise tunes. It was a sadness: he knew there were riches to be had, but they just weren't accessible to him. He'd have to attune himself to the music of the spheres.

He also left behind his novels. That would have been impossible a few years before, but a change had come over him recently. He no longer felt drawn to fiction. If he opened a novel now, even an old favourite, for the first time in his life he was not sucked in. Having spent decades living, it seemed, in other people's worlds, perhaps he now felt the need to live in his own. Maybe that was because a world of his own, instead of one dictated by those around him, now seemed a possibility.

B decided to buy a shredder. If he was going to blot out his past, he needed to do it properly. So, over the period of a week, he shut himself in his room and systematically destroyed the paper record of his life – his bank statements, those from social security, all that documentation that he so disliked. What freedom, to be shot of all that stuff, once and for all. No more paperwork. He paused over his birth certificate. Shredding that would indeed be pretty final, but now he'd got his money he could see no reason why he would ever have to prove his identity to anyone. He existed, whether a paper recorded it or not, and from now on he wanted to keep the fact of his existence to himself. He fed the certificate into the shredder, and watched it disappear.

When all was ready, he fastened the bag, and left it on his bed for later collection.

The highlight of B's days in the ward was the twice-weekly visit of the library trolley. The old biddy who ran it loved her books, and was delighted to find a fellow enthusiast. So many of the inpatients were too ill, or simply not interested in reading. She was amazed by B's capacity for reading and, although B was no longer drawn to fiction, and much of what she had to offer was silly romantic stuff anyway, B could always find something of interest. To his astonishment, one of the books on the trolley was a battered copy of a book about King Arthur and his knights.

What was it about these knights that so resonated with him? As a child they had created a sense of order, of things being in their proper place, of respect for others and self-respect. There was a code of behaviour that was understood. It gave him a sense of settled containment. This, he had thought, is how things ought to be. Modern life, his life, was all over the place. Nobody knew what was what any more. In particular, no one seemed to know – he certainly didn't – what it was to be a man. In his world women ruled the roost.

As an adult, his cherished dream of knighthood was still with him but now somewhat at odds with his newfound Buddhist principles. He had always thought of the knights, especially King Arthur's, as men of chastity, honour and spiritual truth, and he had no problem with that. It was a vision of heroism that filled his dreams: defending his lady-love, with a virtual sword that was a mark of status and honour. However, he couldn't hide the fact that although they didn't seem to have gone on the rampage, or indulged in rape and pillage, the tales of even King Arthur's knights were full of killing. It didn't seem to tally. And they killed not only people, but animals. Sir Percevale himself was said to have killed a snake, but only, B recalled, in order to save a young lion, whose father in turn befriended him, and slept all night at his feet. It was that example of inter-creature friendship that B preferred to remember. His image of knighthood, however ill-defined, was of his own distinctive kind.

Honour and spiritual truth: those were his goals. Chastity? Well, that depended on what you meant. Knights, he had read, were meant to be virtuous, celibate, even. B was not a virgin, technically – he had fumbled himself and one or two random partners to some sort of physical fruition (he shuddered to think of it now) – he certainly had been chaste for some time now, although he conceded that it was more from confusion and lack of opportunity than from any soul-secure resolution.

The library book was not the friend of his childhood, but a version for adults, with longer biographies of each of the main characters. As he looked up the entry for "Sir Percevale", he sat bolt upright in his chair. Before he died, B discovered, Sir Percevale *had become a hermit!* When his close friend and hero, Sir Galahad, died, Percevale had taken holy orders, dying about a year later. Hermit and knight, knight becomes hermit. Was it possible that the two sides of B's Gemini dream-existence had merged? Had always been one? It felt like a sign.

Hamid was the nearest to a friend that he'd ever had. The realisation came as somewhat of a surprise: he had never had any friends to speak of, and Hamid was not the kind of friend B would have imagined. Maybe it was because they were both outsiders. Hamid did not judge; he seemed to accept him as he was, with all his peculiar notions.

On one occasion, when B turned up at the usual café, he was taken aback to discover the young Eritrean was not alone. Initially, B was irritated. The presence of someone else meant they would not be able to continue with their planning. There was a lot to be done, and very little time in which to do it. But the someone else was a young woman and B found it hard not to stare. She was truly beautiful: shy, with long dark hair and dark eyes that lit up when she smiled. Indeed, she herself lit up the room, which took on a sharper clarity in her presence. B was more aware, not only of her faint perfume and the flowery lightness of her dress, but of the shininess of the table and the movement of the air above him from the ceiling fan.

It turned out that Aishe attended the same drop-in centre as Hamid, and was from Poland. Poland? Why would anyone need to seek asylum from Poland? *I am Roma, Gypsy,* she explained. Again, B was astonished: this lovely young woman? She didn't look like any idea he had of a gypsy. She did not look like someone who lived in a caravan. And she didn't. She lived with her extended family, with many other asylum seekers, in a disused hotel in Pinner. Since she was the only member to speak reasonable English, she found herself taking responsibility for her parents, sister, and her own baby. She was trying to start a cake-making business.

But I expect they send me back, she said ruefully. *Your government, they do not believe they treat us badly. They say I lie.*

B was usually in a hurry to be gone, but this time he agreed to have a second cup of coffee, and he bought the other two some sandwiches to be going on with. Absorbed in the rise and fall of her voice in its gently accented English, but most of all basking in her prettiness, he didn't really take in much of the conversation. It didn't occur to him till later that there might have been more between her and Hamid than friendship. All he felt was the beauty of her presence, as an offering to his all-too-eager heart.

In the days that followed, Aishe's fragrant loveliness coloured his waking hours: in his solitude he dreamed of trysts, tender encounters, the meeting of eyes and souls: there was no need for words. A few weeks later B learnt that she had indeed been sent back, and he felt the light dim. Aishe, he remembered, meant "alive", and she had made him feel it. Who would rescue her now?

When the day came, there was only Hamid to witness it. It was only Hamid who'd been there, who knew of his plans, who led the way to his refuge, his retreat. Hamid had reconnoitred the place the previous night, had checked that the electricity had as usual not been actually disconnected, and had done the necessary jerry-rigging of the transfer box, bringing with him a large fuse and copper wire for the purpose. B didn't understand what needed to be done, and wouldn't have known where to start, but Hamid and his friends were old hands at such processes. The Eritrean had then done some food shopping, gone, as asked, to B's house, picked up the packed bag from B's bed, and delivered it all, late at night, to the new place.

He had then come to the hospital during visiting time the following afternoon, and alerted B that the time had come. It was high time, in fact, as the pressure on B to sign a consent form was getting serious. The young man had with him a small rucksack into which he put most of the things B had brought to the hospital, and arranged to meet him downstairs after supper, before the nurses came round with the medicine trolley. B was as usual both amazed at and grateful for Hamid's resourcefulness. He supposed that the life of a non-person demanded creative and secret ways of coping with the challenges of the modern world.

The previous night Hamid had found a way over the wall at the back through a window that he'd manage to loosen. They did not want to alert anyone by breaking in the front door or risk any charges of criminal damage. It would not do to be seen. In winter it got dark long before the ward settled down for the night. B had taken care to keep on the good side of the physios, to practise his exercises in the early evening as a matter of routine, so no one had batted an eyelid at his exit, even with a shoulder bag full of clothes for the outside world. He left on his crutches, their rubber bases squeaking on the impossibly shiny floors, past the nurses, out of the ward, through the double doors to the lifts. On the way down he stared at the floor, not wanting to risk meeting anyone's possibly curious gaze.

How his heart had thumped: fight *and* flight: the flight was a fight – a flight into himself, a fight for his survival as an independent human being. He was terrified of being caught, fearful of the finality of what he was embracing, and yet exhilarated at his courage. For once; he was coming into his own.

After the heavy heat of the ward, it felt very cold outside but, luckily, they didn't have to wait long for the bus. B paid Hamid's fare and used his own Oyster, afterwards proffering the card to Hamid with a slightly embarrassed shrug. He would have no further use for it. It was too early to go to the house – they would have to wait until later to be sure of privacy – so they went to a pub to sit out the first few hours. It had been years since B had been in a pub, and Hamid, who did not drink, had never been in one. It was a good enough place, anonymous and reasonably quiet, with no music or football, just the chat of after-work drinkers. B was glad of the rest, but, clutching his bag, became increasingly twitchy at the delay. He was scared of being caught, scared that somehow "they" would come after him.

At closing time, they left the pub and walked in silence round the corner into a small quiet road. B's attention as he limped along, alternating feet and crutches, was as usual on the ground, careful not to trip over anything, not to slip on the fallen leaves. It was hard for a man who was used to striding out and looking about him, to be reduced to hobbling like an old man. But he was accustomed to it, and tonight his senses were unusually acute, taking in a tree root's triumphant upending of a paving stone, the yellow brilliance of recently fallen leaves, and his breath steaming in the air. When they reached their destination, B waited in the shadows while Hamid went round the back of the building opposite, to climb over the wall. Breathing fast, B contemplated the magnitude of the moment, and for the first time looked up at the sky. Between the buildings and away from the street lamp he could see a few stars and a crescent moon: they gave him a little cheer, as portents of his new life. Almost incidentally he took in the details of his new home: it was a wide old building, about five storeys high, with one of the ground-floor windows boarded up. As a whole it had a pleasing symmetry, but was anonymous and completely dark. He did not expect to see the outside of this building again. He was leaving the world behind.

When the front door opened a crack, B hobbled across the street, through the gate and manoeuvred his crutches gingerly over the broken tiles of the path before pausing on the threshold and glancing back. Hamid pulled him gently into the building, and closed the door behind them. It seemed even colder inside: this was a building that had not been inhabited for a long time. The staircase was of a gracious width. In fact, the whole building had obviously originally been a fine residence, but according to Hamid had been converted some years ago into a mixture of flats and offices. All were empty now, awaiting judgement. A silent sentinel of a building: full, no doubt, of memories, but empty, it appeared, of any present activity.

It was a painfully slow journey as Hamid, torch in hand, led the way across the hall and up dark and dirty stairs to the second floor. Adrenalin kept B going, but he could feel the fear in his mouth as he climbed. He tried to concentrate on the purely physical: good leg, bad leg, crutches, good leg, bad leg, crutches. On the second landing, Hamid reached into the inner pocket of his jacket, and pulled out a plastic card. With focused concentration, he wiggled it in the lock until the door opened, and they were greeted by a billow of warmth. Hamid, bless him, had thought to turn the heating on the night before. He gestured to B to go first, followed him in, and shut the door behind them.

With a whisper, the torch beam pointing at the floor or behind his cupped hand, Hamid showed him round the rooms: pointing out the overnight heaters and the cooker, and switching on the water heater. He had put some basic bedding in one of the rooms, either scrounged from friends or bought when necessary, and bought the first week's provisions with money and from a list B had given him. There were some omissions but B would cope, and learn to forecast his needs better for following weeks. The rooms had basic furniture and some grubby plates and cups and cutlery. It would do. It was his – for the duration.

It was time for Hamid to go. B gave him some money, they shook hands, and then embraced, looking each other gravely in the eye before the young man slipped out. They didn't expect to meet again. B stood without moving in the dark, feeling the stillness, breathing slowly and deliberately, calming himself, centring himself in the unfamiliar space. He then pulled out the brown paper parcel of bank notes from the bag which Hamid had collected the previous night, unwrapped them and, not without irony, spread them out under the mattress. He put his pills and torch next to the bed, and his crutches within easy reach. Extra torch batteries went into the drawer. He went into the bathroom, peed, and removed the little plate with a single tooth from his mouth. After scrubbing it and the rest of his teeth, he placed the plate in a little plastic bag and took it back to the other room. He put it in the drawer. That was something he would never need again. He undressed, unzipped the sleeping bag, and lowered himself on to the bed. He removed his glasses, and lay on his back with his eyes open, gradually adjusting to a fuzzy glimmer of light from the night-time sky. He was there, it was over, it had started. There he was at last: an anchorite: a hermit in the city. A still centre. Pole-axed, he slept.

Chapter 5

B woke the next morning as if from a drugged sleep. He had a sense that the sun had been up for a while – and as he looked around with the usual blurred vision before his spectacles clarified the world, it took a while for him to remember where he was. Now he knew. Safe! He was safe. All those clichés about the first day of the rest of his life.

How glad he was that it was winter, and that the rooms were dark. He wanted nothing more than to burrow down into his snug little place, to wrap himself in the security of long dark nights and the murky gloaming of the days. This was the first morning on which he had woken without a clock. He felt a faint stirring of his habitual anxiety about lateness, that he ought to be doing something, but he lay still till the promptings faded and a wider perspective reclaimed the space. He did not get up straight away, but lay on his back, his arms at his side, and breathed. He delayed entering into the practicalities of the new day, and allowed his mind to wander. He remembered that time long ago in the shared house, and how that had felt like freedom. It felt now like a false dawn. It was as if what's-his-name, Rip van Winkle, had come to for a little, rubbed his eyes, absent-mindedly drunk some more of the liquor, then gone back to sleep again. Now, B was not only awake. He was alive.

Eventually, feeling the pressure of a full bladder, B unzipped the sleeping bag, swung his legs over the edge of the bed in the practised concerted manner, reached for his crutches and, achingly, stood. In the filtered daylight he could take stock of his surroundings. He stood. He sniffed. Was he going mad? The place stank of hospital. Could he have brought that smell with him, on his clothes, perhaps? Then he remembered that Hamid, with little time to spare, had at least sprayed the rooms and applied disinfectant to those areas where it particularly mattered.

There were two rooms, as he'd been told, each with a window: the room he was in looking out to the front, the other with a little kitchenette to the back. The place had an air of abandonment and was pretty filthy. B sighed at the amount of effort it would take to make it habitable, but he had the materials, and there was no time limit. There never would be *ever again*. Time would be measured by the rising and the setting of the sun, and the grumbling of his stomach. There would be no intrusion of deadlines, clocks, or even people. There would be no one to tell him to hurry up or what to do.

Wandering from one room to the other, he saw that, as Hamid had said, all that he needed was there: a cupboard for clothes, another for saucepans and plates. An electric cooker, a fairly ancient bulbous fridge, a worn wooden kitchen table, and another small one that he could move about. Two wooden chairs and a rather dubious dented settee, with broken springs revealed. In the small dark bathroom, the bath was indescribably dirty. B couldn't imagine that he'd ever use it – getting in and out of a bath was pretty impossible these days – but there was a loo and a basin, sufficient for his needs. Most of all, there were storage heaters and hot water. How could he be so lucky!

For the first few days there was too much to do to think very much about anything. After years of exposure to near-sterile environments in hospital, at the vet's surgery, and even in his parents' home, where he used to imagine germs fleeing from Mother's rubber gloves, it was extraordinary to be somewhere that was, frankly, disgusting. Although he had enjoyed the relaxed attitude to cleaning in the shared house, and took a large part of responsibility for the gradually accumulated grime, this level of dirt was an altogether different kettle of fish. But once sorted, the place wouldn't need much upkeep. There was only him. And, in any case, this was different. This was his – he was tempted to say – his sacred space.

B set about cleaning as best he could. The kitchen above all: scrubbing the surfaces, the sink, and mopping the floor with a cloth on the end of the broom. In the main rooms too he scrubbed the tables and the wooden chairs, wiping every other wipeable surface. He observed that he was once again plunged into scrubbing. What was all this about? First the surgery, and now this. Had he been a dung beetle in a previous life? Well, all this physical activity kept him warm at least. In the afternoon, before the heat came on, he opened the back window to let freezing cold air into a space that had been enclosed for God knew how long, and he kept moving so that his muscles would not seize up in the cold.

When he felt the heat rise into the air, he shut the window and collapsed on to one of the wooden chairs. He was exhausted by the unfamiliar exercise, but also in a stupor, trying to take in what had happened. That all his plans and dreams had come to fruition was astonishing, so why did he not feel the exhilaration? Tiredness had a lot to do with it, of course, but he had to admit that there was also a sense of anti-climax. He'd done it; he was here. But, now what?

B had no idea where he was. For a Londoner born and bred, B knew very little of the city. He knew his patch in the suburbs, where he had lived and gone to school; he had come to know a little bit of the East End, the route from home to work; and the well-trodden paths of his customary running routes. On the odd occasions when he and Mother had ventured into central London, it had been for shopping in the West End. They had gone by tube, and just popped up near Oxford Street. Those were outings he preferred to forget, and he had no idea about anywhere else. After the accident he had been transferred to a central hospital with more expertise in dealing with complex fractures, but he had no idea where it was in relation to anything else. So, as far as he was concerned, where he was now existed in a vacuum.

And, for the first couple of days, he did not explore the outside world. He had enough to keep him occupied in sorting himself out, and he deliberately kept away from the front windows. He did not want to see the world go by. He wanted to know these rooms, to feel that he was here. The outside, whatever it was, could wait. For now he was here, and the rest of the world could go hang.

B was surprised by how much time just the ordinary activities of the day took. Cooking, washing up and his daily routines of washing, exercise and meditation took much of his time and energy. The hours of daylight were short. Despite the habitual pain, within minutes of zipping the sleeping bag around him, he sank into a dreamless sleep.

The contrast between these surroundings and what he'd left behind couldn't have been more stark. Gone were the glaring white lights of the hospital. Gone too was the constant noise of the ward. Nights filled by the bleep of monitors, the chat of the nurses, and the grunts, groans and snores of his fellow-patients, and sometimes a shout or gabble in an undecipherable language. Here, B woke to a twilight gloom and the soothing balm of near-silence.

B found that he wasn't very good at fending for himself. Even before his accident, when he lived with Malcolm and Tony, he'd found it a trial but now the problems were altogether of a different magnitude. He realised how he had taken for granted the helping hand that was usually available from his family, however grudgingly given and ungraciously received, and of course in hospital everything had been done for him. He had resented being reliant on others, but had hugely underestimated the physical difficulties of living on his own.

In particular, he just hadn't appreciated how hard it would be, coping with crutches by himself. He could just about pick big things up from the floor, by leaning on a chair, putting his right leg behind him and bending his good leg, but mostly he relied on his faithful litter pick, the wonderful device OT had given him years ago when he left hospital the first time. More recently, he'd been able to put his weight down a bit – indeed was encouraged to do so to help bone growth – and manage with one crutch when necessary but, even so, he hadn't realised the number of tasks that needed the use of two hands. In the kitchen he could do without the crutches, moving himself around the units; in the bathroom too, he could lean on the basin, leaving both his hands free. It was carrying things from one place to another that was perilous, so he'd taken to eating out of a large bowl, to avoid spilling food on his jerky travels to the other room. When pain made the use of both crutches necessary, he slung a carrier bag round his wrist, in which he could carry any number of things. He avoided the soppy little cups and saucers in the cupboard, and got Hamid to buy him a couple of mugs, in which drinks could be kept secure by the application of cling film across the top: a really good tip one of the other patients had given him. Independence was a wonderful thing, but no one could say it was easy.

By the time he was admitted to hospital for the last time, he'd had the external frame for some months, and was pretty used to coping with it. He couldn't bear to dwell on how the pins were attached to his leg. If he pictured what it was actually like, he began to feel faintly sick. The frame was heavy, and it made him clumsy all over again – a constant reminder of his innate awkwardness that he'd fought so hard to overcome. He could not afford to be clumsy now. If he spilt or dropped things, clearing them up was no easy matter. When he dropped a bag of nuts and they rolled all over the floor, he had to use his trusty litter pick to pick them up one by one. He schooled himself to treat such incidents as an amusing opportunity for mindfulness, but when he was tired it was not such fun, and he realised how used he had got to people picking things up for him.

The other troubling reminder of a discarded childhood self was the fact that his custom-made trousers had been torn by the frame, and were now full of holes and pulled threads. As a teenager he couldn't have cared less about tatty clothes. Now he was forced to care because there was no way that he could get any new specially adapted trousers. He would have to ask Hamid to buy some size-18 jogging bottoms, and pull the draw strings tight around his waist. Thankfully he'd never cared much about clothes: these specially capacious trousers were certainly not a fashion item. He was thankful too that he'd not had foot rings fitted, which apparently caused a lot of grief in finding footwear and in walking itself. When he cursed the bulk and rigidity of the frame, he had to remind himself that without it he would be lost, all independence gone.

B had his daily exercises to stretch the leg and ankle and keep the knee mobile, and had established a meticulous and lengthy cleaning routine of the pin sites. This was the most trying part of his daily routine (twice-daily, in fact), but he didn't dare skimp it. The last thing he needed was an infection. Without a mirror, of course, it was hard to ensure he had cleaned the pin sites at the back of his leg. Even twisting as much as he could, he was not able to bend the leg up to look at it properly. Fingers crossed.

Even washing his feet was a problem. Not that he minded that much, but it had to be done occasionally, and there was no way he could get his feet anywhere near the basin. Eventually he got Hamid to get him a washing-up bowl. He had used one at Mother's, and had made the mistake of putting it on the floor, only to find that there was no way he could lift the bowl, and of course the litter pick was of no use with that kind of weight. He had stared at the bowl of water, and wondered what on earth he could do. Gritting his teeth, he painstakingly used his litter pick to grip a small plastic tub and baled some of the water, little by little, from the bowl and tipped it into the basin. But still some remained, and he was forced to leave the increasingly stagnant water until he could bear to ask Mother for help. Now that he was alone, there was no help to be had, so he put the bowl on a little pile of books and, with a jug from the kitchen, he half-filled it with hot water. He then sat on the loo seat and soaked his poor feet, relishing the soothing heat. He couldn't bend his right leg very far, but by putting the towel on the floor and using his left foot to wrap it round his right before standing up and stamping on it, it was more or less job done.

B trimmed his hair from time to time with a pair of scissors, although he had no way of telling whether he'd managed to keep a straight line. His beard too. His beard! Without a mirror he wasn't able to shave. His only attempt had been a bloody experiment. Once the stubble had gone beyond the scratchy, itchy stage, the beard was all right. It took some getting used to, but then it became a liberation: no more shaving, ever. He had never been keen on the hippy look, had always had quite a conservative image in his clothes and hairstyle but now that was how it had to be. Maybe he really was Rip van Winkle! He'd never actually seen the whole of his beard, only the end which was within the orbit of his sight. Now, strangely, since there was no one to see it, and it didn't matter, he took care when he was eating, wiped his mouth, was careful that no food got stuck in his beard. It was bad enough having a long, hippy-like beard without there being bits of food it in it. That really would have been gross. It was probably just as well that he couldn't see himself as he was now. His appearance was bound to be a shock, so when it was dark he took care when approaching the window at the back that there was no light behind him.

It would have been easy to become a slob. Sometimes the temptation not to wash, not to do his exercises, not to do anything, in fact, was almost overwhelming. Only the inbuilt discipline of his routine, and the fear of complete disintegration, kept him on course. Such licence as he allowed himself was consciously done. When his hands were mucky, if it was too difficult to get to the sink he just wiped his hands on his trousers. Anyway, he washed his own clothes, so Mother *could just shut up*.

Now that he lived on his own, B was careful to look after himself with dietary supplements for his joints and bones, and a balanced diet. He couldn't be tempted by junk food, because he couldn't go out and get it. The cool-headed creation of a shopping list each week was not made in the same mindset as the addictive need to guzzle, and soon the cravings for burgers or sticky buns faded. In fact, after the feeble and repetitive excuse for a veggie diet provided by the hospital, it was a joy to eat real food: fresh veg, pulses, above all, rice, which had become something of a staple. He could choose what and when to eat, and re-visit some of the discoveries he had made in the shared house.

Trying to keep fit, however, was a losing battle. Despite the exercises it was hard to tire himself physically, and he knew that being indoors all the time couldn't be good for him. Whatever the weather, he made a point of spending a few minutes every day with the back window open, taking deep breaths of the freshest air that the centre of a city could offer. He was aware of the danger of hypochondria, wryly remembering the scene from some book he'd read in his early teens, where the characters convinced themselves they had every disease imaginable. At least he could no longer look up real or imaginary symptoms on the net. That way madness lay. And he knew that with this kind of isolated life, madness could be just around the corner. He hoped that the discipline of his regular routine would guard against a descent into depression or losing it altogether.

But he managed to keep healthy. Living alone did at least mean that he never came into contact with viruses. During the time he'd been in these rooms he had not suffered so much as a cough. He lived with pain, and his body was no doubt deteriorating, but he held the decline at bay as best he could. He could not afford to be ill.

In all but the coldest weather, B slept naked. With his leg-frame protected by a cut-off pyjama leg, there was little to catch on it, and in any case he loved the silkiness of the sleeping bag against his body, loving even more the frisson of forbiddenness that had been instilled by years of obedience, even acquiescence, to his mother's strictures. He marvelled at how long he had allowed her influence to hold sway, even from beyond the grave. The way she went on, you'd have thought that nudity was a cardinal sin. It was now as if he were loosening her clutches on him, prising her gnarled fingers open, one by one. In this cell of his own choosing he was releasing himself from oppression.

As B reclaimed his mind and his will he was beginning to realise the importance of the body: that was where the Christians had got it wrong. *We have bodies for a reason,* he thought, *like animals, connected to the earth.* For some years now, practising meditation, sitting, concentrating on his breathing, his feet on the floor, his bum on the chair, he had begun to acquire a happier sense of unity with his body, to reclaim a body which he had been brought to believe was somehow dirty, impure, especially those parts which his mother, with an embarrassed twist of the mouth, would refer to as *down there.* He could now openly acknowledge the satisfaction of an eye-wateringly good crap. He'd once heard someone talking about an elderly couple, saying that the fact that they counted their own faeces was a sure sign of neurosis. Did that make him a neurotic? He was more aware, too of his smell. He wondered if he would seem to smell to others. If he was on a bus (not that he was ever likely to be now) would he become one of those smelly old men that everyone changed seats to avoid, breathing through their mouths when passing by? He wasn't dirty: he washed, but he was more aware of the smell of his armpits, his prick – he *liked* his smell. It was part of him. Even his veggie farts. Oh, the luxury of letting rip! And he liked the taste of his cock too: transferred by hand, he was no contortionist! Was this what a woman would – no, no, no, no – as he felt himself aroused, don't go there.

B longed for the utter lack of self-consciousness of an animal, or a small child. It wasn't surprising that actors were warned not to appear with either of them. They were bound to win the hearts of the audience. Some had more charisma than others, but much of their charm came from a directness unblinkered by pretence. They were true. Not all of them, of course. There were dogs that had been taught to jump through hoops, and children too, blighted by parental expectation. Like Ella, but not like Vicky, or Jeff – or himself, come to that. It had taken a long time to break down his resistance.

Did he remember that innocent unselfconscious state? He had a sense that that stage had gone on longer with him than with most children; perhaps that was one of the reasons he had never fitted in. Now that there was no one to observe him, he had hoped that self-consciousness would disappear altogether, but almost the reverse seemed to be true. There was too little to distract him from himself. He was conscious of the noises he made: a cough, a sneeze, or the sound of his munching as he ate. The least sound reverberated in the emptiness. Only by focusing his full attention on something, no matter what, could he achieve oblivion for a while. But there was nothing approaching the ecstasy of self-forgetfulness that the experience of running had brought him.

Part of the Buddhist teaching was to try to lead a life that was less sense-dependent but, actually, he found that deprivation, and an attempt to be aware of his surroundings, made him more aware, more reliant on his senses. One day, as he ate his lunch, staring dreamily into space, he rubbed his thumb along the ridge under the table-top, feeling the pleasing unevenness of the wood, the knots, the roughness a contrast with any laminate smoothness. Feeling – ugh! What was that? He withdrew his hand sharply, his thumb coated in some greyish gunge. For God's sake! Not chewing gum – that would have hardened – but some kind of slime. He didn't need that sort of reminder of human activity. God knew how long it had been there. B limped to the bathroom, let the hot water run, and scrubbed his hands till all traces of the disgusting substance were gone.

Although he liked his smell, he knew that when his bedding got too pongy, it needed a wash. Thank God Hamid had got him a sleeping bag. Changing sheets would have been tough; he'd had to do it at Mother's, so he knew. Stripping the bed was easy enough, but lifting the mattress, bending and tucking in the sheets had been painful and, requiring both hands, de-stabil-ising. His sleeping bag didn't get washed often, but at least now that the heating was on, there was some way of drying it. So, in the winter it got washed; in warmer weather it probably wouldn't. Washing it wasn't much fun, anyway. Squashing it into the kitchen sink (it was bigger than the basin), the endless rinsing to get the soap out, and the wringing till his hands hurt before hanging it over a string line over the otherwise unused bath until the drips had stopped. Even when the heaters were on, you couldn't cover them with anything, so there was no other way to dry his clothes or bedding except to drape them over every other possible surface: the tops of doors, or over the furniture. The rooms were continually draped with damp, and damp-smelling, material. He had to be careful not to walk into a curtain of washing at night. He couldn't afford a fall, and for that reason, however tiresome, in the dark he put on his glasses, and used both crutches.

Night-time activities had always been a secret pleasure: a time when no one – not Annette, not Mother – knew what he was up to. Never mind how insignificant it was: reading a book or scratching his arse, it was something hidden and somehow unlicensed, naughty, something he did for himself alone. So even now that no one could forbid him anything, any nocturnal activity felt like a bonus, something stolen. One of the things he often did at night now was write his journal. He took pleasure in every aspect of it: the feel of the little cloth-bound book, opening it up, the whiteness of the new page, the sound of his pencil on the paper. To begin with, it had seemed important to record everything factually and truthfully, then, as there were fewer and fewer new activities to record, his thoughts, emotions, dreams and stories took over. Initially, he scrupulously wrote down all the details of his dreams, knowing them to be an aid to wisdom, a possible resource, but, as time went on, sitting up with his torch to write them down just seemed too much of an effort. As always, he enjoyed doodling. He sometimes dwelt on the letter of the following day (or was it already that day? He would never know) until he fell asleep. Sometimes it was hard, especially in winter, to know when a broken night ended and a new day began, to know when it was time to get up.

He didn't usually turn on his torch for nocturnal peeing – there was enough light from the street – but when he wished to write, he took pleasure in its light, carefully angled down with its sharp bright circle of light at the centre, with a dark circle within, and the paler shade of its wider penumbra. One night, he shone it on his hand, holding the torch up close, and studying his veins, his pores, and the way the hairs grew. Suddenly tired, he turned off the torch, lay back down and tried to relax. B had long schooled himself to lie on his back. It was not his normal position, but since the accident he was unable to lie in any other way. How he longed for the more abandoned postures of his youth. It was yet another example of his continuing imprisonment. Even without Mother, he was trapped. Where was freedom?

Once the novelty of his new life wore off, B became bored. He wasn't by nature a person of routine, and he found its effects somewhat deadening. He tried to vary what he did – putting on the right sock before the left, putting fruit on his cereal before the milk – but there was little scope in an existence bounded by his injury and the self-imposed mindful pattern of his life. Change the pen he used for his diary? No, that was a step too far. Once or twice he'd tried writing with his right hand: that was certainly slow and mindful though the outcome was pretty dire. The need for his natural spontaneity began to push against the confines of his imposed discipline.

Once he had done his morning meditation, his exercises, and gone for his "walk" at the front window, he paced up and down, fiddled with his books, and tried to think of things – games, any kind of distraction – to fill the interminable time of the longer days. He started the alphabet game, set himself goals: seeing how long he could stand on one leg, how long he could hold his breath. In his more expansive life back in the world, when he first stopped watching TV, it was mainly because there was nothing he wanted to watch, and he was fed up with wasting his time. But he had never solved the problem of what to do with his evenings. Here, of course, the problem was magnified. If he did not relax before going to bed his mind would not stop, and usually by the end of the day he had had enough of pondering, reading and meditation. There had to be, he knew, something to occupy his down-time. What could it be? In his preparations, B had stored up some thousand-piece jigsaws, which had stood him in reasonable stead, especially after turning the cover picture down. Crosswords would have been lighter and easier to carry but, despite his love of words, B had never really got on with them. He didn't retain facts easily, so his general knowledge was poor, and apt to be shown up by those supposedly simple puzzles; and, as for the cryptic variety, he simply didn't know where to begin. Didn't see the point of all that mystification anyway.

One evening, for want of anything better, he got one of the jigsaws out, and started it again, face down, seeing if he could identify the place just by the shape of the piece, then discarded it in irritation. It wasn't this kind of elderly, invalid activity that he was looking for. He hobbled around the rooms, feeling trapped.

He was sick of his routine, sick of being so ruddy careful, sick of always paying attention: surely there was more to life than this? He longed to be careless, carefree; most of all he longed to run.

After a few days of intense frustration, because there was nothing that he could do about it, and because regular meditation had begun to have an effect, B gradually succumbed to a kind of acceptance and calm. Tension dropped from his shoulders, and he began to breathe with a freedom that was new. He began to believe that this was his space, that he could be here and left alone. That no one would enter his space, tell him he shouldn't be there, shouldn't do that, shouldn't be who he was. He realised that Mother's insistent voice was bullying him no longer. Her presence had faded, and with it much of the pain of his past. He began to believe in peace, and in himself. He stopped fretting. It simply didn't matter. He remembered that as a child he'd been bewildered by all the anxiety that people had about things that didn't seem important. Inevitably he'd absorbed some of it, but now he happily returned to his old views, shrugging off the overlay of others' completely unimportant concerns. They didn't matter. They never had mattered. He had been right all along.

Chapter 6

Spring was on its way. B had no idea of the date, not that it mattered, but the sun was higher in the sky and, when he pushed up the back window, he sniffed a warmer air, air that even in the centre of London carried a richer scent. Soon, buds would appear on the plane trees at the front; there would be a burgeoning of life in all its leafy greenness. Now that the weather was warmer, he was able to leave the window open for longer. Although it opened on to a brick-and-concrete blankness, a different energy seemed to enter the rooms. Another winter survived.

Outside the back window was not a sheer drop. The floor under his extended a little way, so there was a little gulley below him where rainwater sometimes collected for a while before it drained away. There was some there now from the night's rain and, as he stood at the open window, he glanced down. There, there was no mistaking it, was growing a pansy. Extraordinary! B drank in the richness of its little face with the avidity of a starving man. Its little light-yellow central "eye" was surrounded by deep-purple velvet edged by a paler shade, its surface glistening under a covering of droplets. Even as he watched, a large raindrop, as if discovering that it was too heavy for the feminine grace of the pansy face, slipped off, and, relieved of the weight, the flower sprang back up. B longed to touch it, but had to be content with gazing at it from above, taking in its delicate presence as part of his daily "walk". The seed must have been carried by the wind. Fancy that! All that way from some more fertile spot. Nature had a way of invading even the most desolate of man-made structures. Provide a crack, B thought, and something living will find it and fill it.

B stood still and became aware of his breath, and a breath connection with the little plant. *We need their oxygen to breathe in,* he thought *and, strangely – CO2 has such a bad press – they need us to breathe out.* Maybe the same creative wind that had brought the pansy to his little ledge outside was now blowing into these rooms.

For once B felt the pain of his solitude. He was used to being alone – indeed, was all too aware of the dangers of association – but the wish to share sometimes swept over him. He was long used to barricading his heart. It came as second nature but occasionally the piercing of a chink like this caught him unawares. Into the chink entered all the living companions of his life. If only he could have a dog, he would be content. Or a cat, or a hamster, or even a fish. But he would never condemn any living creature to this existence.

Unusually, he'd woken that morning with a feeling of deep content. He'd gained consciousness slowly, languorously, aware that for once he'd not woken in the night. Aware too that he was not in pain. Slowly, working his way from his toes to his head, he gave attention to every part of his body as it touched the bed; he stretched, then relaxed and lay quietly, immensely grateful for the respite. As he played idly with his flaccid cock, he had a flash of memory of himself in the bath, aged about four. He was playing with his cock then, too, fascinated by the sight of it bobbing on the water. And then Mother had come into the room and caught him at it. B smiled at the memory of her scandalised face. No such problem now.

The wakening respite didn't last long. When he finally got to his feet, his old enemy reasserted its presence in his joints and muscles. He could tell as soon as he put weight on his leg that this was going to be a two-crutch day, and he reached for his paracetamol. But the feeling of peace seemed to have seeped deeper, into his bones, so he was able to continue calmly with his morning routine.

He decided to treat himself to a fry-up. His shopping had arrived the night before, so there were fresh mushrooms and tomatoes as well as baked beans. It was one of the few times that he missed meat. A fry-up was a poor thing without sausages or bacon, but nonetheless a refreshing change from his daily fare of muesli, which he'd always thought a poncey sort of breakfast, even if he knew that as a vegetarian he needed the cereals and nuts. After clearing up he settled gratefully in his chair facing the wall. He set his timer, removed his glasses, closed his eyes and focused on his breathing.

It was strange how, when he first arrived, B had been so struck by the silence. Now, he was acutely aware of the noise: outside, the faint sound of a car alarm or an aeroplane; a distant siren announcing that help was on its way, maybe, to some other poor sod. From inside the flat, he could hear the hum of the fridge, and nearer to home, the sound of his steps as he hobbled around, the rustling of a bag or turning of a page, the sound of his own breathing, even the clicking of his bones. One of the earliest introductions to meditation that he had learnt was to listen to the sounds far away, then bring the attention into the room, then to one's own breath. And stay there, with the breathing. Not hard to do when there were relatively so few sounds. But silence there was not.

Meditation was unpredictable. The whole process, after all, was a surrender to the unknown, so it was not surprising that he should sometimes be taken unawares. In general, if he was able to banish the monkey mind and settle into a peaceful state, the outcome too was peaceful, a state in which he could face with equanimity pain, and the other realities of his life. But, in long sessions, he often fought to stay awake, fought to stay still within the discipline of the process. Fought against shouting his frustration, fought, in fact, with his wish to throw it all up, give in to his life-long habit of escape.

But, that morning, his battle with self transmuted into something else. As he forced himself to stay with the process, he found himself in another place, breath quickened, a molten gold covering all. All thought, words, material life, dissolved. It was as if a dazzling light pervaded his soul. Opening his eyes, B immediately began another round, and found all imbued with a new intensity, he *saw* the bricks and mortar of the wall as if never before. And then all faded, the humdrum and fatigue returned, and all was as it had been. So, that was what it was all about. At last he knew experientially what he had so often read about. A warm surge of gratitude flooded through his veins.

As he lay on his bed that evening, he felt affirmed in the choice he had made. There was no doubting it, in the struggle between the two sides of himself, it was the hermit that had won through. It was a side of himself that had always been with him, had always made being in the world so hard. In fact, when he looked back, his life reminded him of the hermit picture in his gran's attic. It was grey. Such contrasts as there were had been in low relief. Only occasionally had his life burst into colour: the moment of fury when he had punched the bully at school, and the joy of running: oh yes, that was an experience of blazing colour. And now he was consolidating that calmer life. It was a grey existence, maybe, but one free of the agitation that had so troubled him in his earlier life. Peaceful, serene, infinitely preferable.

As for any vision of heroism, he had had to let it go. There was no room for his hero-self in this solitary life. Only in stoicism, in overcoming pain, only to himself could he be a hero. Maybe that was the point. There was no room to express his heroism in the wider world: it was a world in which he played no part. An outlaw and a solitary, he had to let go of that part of himself, or so he told himself. He wasn't always sure that his self was listening.

B had never told anyone of his day dreams. Whom could he have told? When he was little, he had chatted a little to his gran, and no doubt she could have guessed from his shiny eyes a little of his passion. But in all those lonely years since her death there had been no confidant. He wondered if he might have confided in Hamid, the only person who seemed prepared to listen and who, it came to him, was as near a perfect gentle knight as anyone he had ever met. But he had missed the opportunity. No one would hear about what mattered to him now.

It wasn't that B regretted his decision. Not at all. How could he? What choice had he had? There had been but one: amputation and going to live with bossy Annette, putting himself once again under the power of a domineering woman. He'd rather die. It had been extraordinary to realise that even the accident was not a source of regret. However reluctantly, he had to acknowledge the truth of the Buddhists' understanding of suffering as a lesson. He could not deny that it had been through that breaking of his body that he had found his way. He detested his helplessness, yes, but knew too that his life before the accident had been pretty stuck in a different kind of helplessness.

Even when he'd been living with Tony and Malcolm, the time he nicknamed "The Years of Independence", he'd been stuck. No, he had needed a clean break (so to speak). If he had any regrets, it was that he had no animal there to share his life. He missed the contact with living beings that he'd had at the surgery and the sense that he could make a difference, that there was a way in which that tender part of him, exposed so late and with such fear, could be expressed.

How B wished he could control the state of his awakening. No matter how serene he was when he fell asleep, how well prepared for the night, no matter how relatively pain-free he felt, how he was when he woke up was completely unpredictable. Sometimes he would wake feeling settled in himself, calm and at ease; at other times he was depressed, and it would take quite a time to shake himself out of it, or twitchy and pre-occupied with his physical condition. Sometimes he came to with a jerk, a sudden awakening, propelled into the conscious world as if summoned by some emergency. Sometimes he woke immersed in a delightful sensuous lethargy. Maybe he'd slept for longer, or more deeply. Just better, anyhow and, from that rested place, he could face even the onset of pain with optimism. He wondered how much of it had to do with planetary activity. He wished he had studied astrology more seriously while he had the chance; it might have helped make more sense of an inner self that seemed to be tugged by invisible forces.

B did believe in the power of the planets. Not in that silly way that Annette did, through reading her horoscope every day in the paper, but, given the proven impact of the moon on tides, and its obvious effect on animals and some sensitive people, "lunatics", it made sense. *After all,* he thought, *we are all part of the same firmament, intimately connected, why wouldn't the movement of the planets have some effect on us?*

Some of the turbulence of his moods found expression in his dreams. Although B increasingly felt that he was gaining some mindful mastery over his wayward life, a state for which he'd dreamed and worked, he could not control what happened in his sleep, when there exploded into his night-time consciousness a colourful kaleidoscope of shapes and sensations. Frocks and frills, tits and smiles, children and animals tumbled helter-skelter through his dreams. He was exhilarated. He ran, he jumped and skipped. *Look at me,* he shouted, *I can dance!* It was in his dreams that he found his legs and his voice.

He also found his sexual power. In general, sex, or the lack of it, was less of a problem these days. Gone were the days of torment as he walked the streets or rode on the tube, forever faced by couples kissing and fondling, girls with legs and the curve of breasts revealed. Averting his eyes, his heart and prick pumping blood. A quick wank on his return was a necessary release. It still was, sometimes, but less often. Getting a bit older definitely helped, and he was sure that a meat-free diet made it all a bit easier to control: not ingesting all that hormone-fed flesh, the panic of a butchered animal feeding into its blood. Less protein altogether, really. Calmer, more in control. He liked to think that he was bodily aware, no longer driven.

That was during the day. His night-time activity was another matter. Whereas his day dreams were largely idealistic, his dreams at night were usually unashamedly earthy, and he often woke with an erection. When he was younger, these morning erections had been a shameful embarrassment. Now, casting off Mother's uglification of all things sexual (how did she come to produce himself and Annette?) he could take some pride in an upright cock. And now the question was whether to wank, to pee, or to ignore it? What was the point of an erection, with nowhere to go? Whenever he imagined that he was in control, he had only to think of these unsought erections – such a trial in the past – to know that he was not. It did not need outside forces to humble him; his own body could do that for him.

Sometimes the hectic activity of his dreams left him exhausted. Sometimes when he woke his heart was thumping. Waking from dreams in which he was always fit and healthy momentarily gave B hope of a returning wholeness, but he was soon brought home to a horrible realisation of the gap between the dream and the waking "reality", if that was what it was. His night-time existence was so much keener, more vivid, than what passed for reality in his waking hours. Day and night, dream and "reality": he half-heartedly hung on to the divisions, fearing that sanity would go if he gave into the blurring of boundaries he increasingly felt were artificial. Surely, they were parallel worlds.

In his more reflective moments, B realised with shame that his newfound compassion did not extend to human beings. People in general, yes: he wished no one any harm and had tried to lead a peaceable life, but the thoughts of his family were far from peaceable, and he knew in his head that it was something to work on in his meditations. But it had not yet reached his heart, and that lack of peace was one of the things that disturbed his sleep.

One morning B woke convulsed with anger of a shocking intensity. But this time it was not at his mother, but about his father. B had loved his father so much, had wanted him to be there for him, to be a real man, a real role model, a real dad to him. And he hadn't, he hadn't. *Why did you die? Why did you never talk to me? Never take my side, never protect me?* B beat his head against the headboard in sheer frustration and pain. What had he ever done wrong? He had tried so hard, but nothing had ever been enough not only to please Mother, but to jerk his father out of his self-contained muteness. B could barely formulate the thought that came to him. His father was not the man he had looked up to, had hero-worshipped: he was not wise, he was weak, he was – a *coward.* The shock of the discovery and of enunciating the word left B gasping.

He lurched out of bed, feeling completely out of control. He normally managed to keep his temper under lock and key, but now it threatened to erupt, with no avenue for expression. No running for him now. How could he possibly express his fury *silently*? The need for silence had long been oppressive, and in this moment it was well nigh intolerable. As he took his bowl and cutlery from the draining board, he shook with the effort to control himself. He longed to clink, to clatter, to bang, to shout, *to make a noise.* But still his fear of discovery damped him down. In a life used to constraint, his self-imposed discipline won through. But he was shaky. Managing his crutches, keeping on his feet, was as much as he could do. Everything felt insecure.

As B went through the usual motions of the day, the shock stayed with him, as did a weakness that supplanted the anger as it drained away. After washing up, he sat with a coffee, trying to recover, then forced himself to go to his meditation spot, set his timer, and sit in the usual way. But he couldn't concentrate. Unsettling images floated across his closed eyelids. He had to keep stopping, acknowledging the distraction and starting again.

The images were, above all, of the face of his mother. Not the face he had lived with, but the unfamiliar face that he had seen in the coffin. Like a reproach, it came again and again. He couldn't imagine such a face in life, smiling and serene. But who was to say that it hadn't existed, that gentler self. Others seemed not to have a problem with her. Maybe it *was* all his fault.

Leave it. Let it go. BREATHE.

Meeting Hamid, and Aishe, had revolutionised his thinking, even more now when the life he was living was not so different from those down and outs he'd been brought up to despise. Only now could he stand back and recognise, despite his constant battles with his mother, just how many of her attitudes he had unconsciously absorbed. It was a painful admission, and one that would have astonished his mother. He knew she had been disappointed in him. She had died thinking him a failure. Just as well she couldn't see him now: she'd have had a fit. He wondered what his father would have thought. Much the same, probably, though in his usual way he would probably have blamed himself.

LEAVE it. Let it pass. He struggled to calm his mind and bring his attention back, once again, to the breath.

But he didn't go along with all that guilt stuff, did he? Self-examination, reflection, yes, acknowledgement, yes. Sorry. Move on. Try not to do it again. But all that self-flagellation – physical or emotional – forget it. It was negative and unhelpful. It did not have to be part of a hermit's life.

B was preparing his supper when he heard the sweet song again. It had been about a month ago, when he was making his early morning cup of tea that he had first heard it. Then, as now, he had stopped in his tracks. Surely he must be mistaken? He turned off the kettle and into the usual silence of the barren bricks outside came, unmistakeably, the sound of a bird, a – could it be? – a blackbird. He had craned his head out and seen a crescent moon in the early morning sky, cradling what he presumed was Venus – a planet, certainly. Then he saw it: a black dot high up on the roof of an office block to his right, on the rail of what looked like the frame of high diving boards but he assumed was some kind of fire escape. How he wished he'd kept his binoculars. Yes, there it was, a blackbird. What joy! The only birds he'd ever seen till then were pigeons, and although he tried to think kindly of them, to be frank he found them pretty ugly. A nice mother-of-pearl sort of sheen on the neck, engaging pink toes and busy little steps, but stolid, podgy, ungainly, somehow unbirdlike birds.

In the old days the presence of a blackbird would have meant nothing to B, but in this creature-starved universe, his heart had risen with gratitude that first time, as it did now. It was singing its heart out. How did such a small body create such a sound? Confident, self-possessed, completely unaware of its audience for whom, like a green shoot in the desert, it was a kind of salvation. The song rang out in the clarity of the twilight air.

Now that the weather was warmer, B could sit in meditation for longer. Increasingly, after the timed session had finished, he continued to sit. He was physically at ease: a rare state for him these days. At ease too in his mind and spirit. He had let go of anxiety, regret, the need to do or be anything. Just sitting, just being, resting in awareness, in a greater sense of spaciousness, within and without. In the end he stopped timing his sessions at all. Now that the need to impose that discipline on himself had gone, he could just sit until cold or an increasing stiffness brought him literally to his senses. When he was in the groove, he found it hard to stop. And there was no need to, despite the nudge of his habitual puritanical objection. This was what he was here to do.

But with his growing ease with meditation came a restlessness. The coming of spring, and the fancy of a still young man turning to love, or lust, or just the sap rising, and energy returning to the body. How strong the life force was! The need to get up, to get going, even when there was nothing to get going at, no need to do anything. It wasn't just habit, or hunger or a need to pee, it was a powerful urge to respond to his body and muscles shouting at him to get on with the day.

Life meant movement. In these rooms, nothing moved, there was no life except his own, no movement unless he made it happen, and sometimes, for the sake of it, he wiggled a wrist, drummed his fingers, kicked his good leg up and down. Sometimes, he was caught by surprise by the glimpse of a part of him moving, as if it belonged to someone else. Only by turning to the front window would he see the movement of other forms: human, bird and, sometimes, in the distance, the trees.

One night B simply couldn't sleep. He wriggled in the sleeping bag, unable to find a comfortable position. Not only was his leg aching; his "bad" foot was itching too. An intolerable itch, made worse by not being able to reach to scratch it. You'd expect a minor irritation to be blotted out by pain, but it was quite the opposite: one thing built on another, it was all just too bloody much. He knew he had some bites: he'd seen them on his stomach. Some living being had managed to enter his sanctuary after all, even if he'd never seen it. He unzipped the sleeping bag, and hobbled around the room, stamping his foot and searching for any kind of implement that would soothe the itch – anything with a long handle would do. His litter pick, if he could find it. He remembered hearing how even amputated legs hurt, twitched or itched, even when there was nothing there. Odd tricks one's nerves played. But amputation was something he didn't want to think about.

When B woke and put on his glasses, patterns of light were already dancing on the wall next to him. Was it his imagination, or was daytime reaching its peak? It was hard to tell, but the sun seemed to have more power. B was so used to the dull light of winter and the twilight zone of his rooms, that not only did the increasingly bright days come as a surprise, but looking out of the window actually hurt his eyes. He was turning into a mole. He wondered if it was some time near his birthday. Ironic that he should have been born in the height of the season of light, whereas Annette, sunny Annette, had arrived in the depths of winter. Maybe the character of each compensated for the season in which they had been born.

His birthday last year had fallen during the Jubilee. Not that it was something that had bothered him one way or another, but all that patriotic fervour had brought vividly to mind his dad, who very oddly used to cry when the National Anthem was played on the radio. It wasn't that he'd been fascinated by the royals: he did not, for instance, go gaga when Princess Di died, the way some of the neighbours did. He'd never dared ask, but B thought it must have been something about his country, identifying with all that was noble, heroic, or that was how B liked to read it.

Annette and the girls had been excited by the celebrations, of course, coming down for the day to wave their flags in the pouring rain. B gathered that like most people they'd been stuck behind crowds, and Ella had cried because she couldn't see any of the boats, but they all agreed they'd had a great time. Chance of a lifetime, wasn't it? As he'd been out of hospital at the time, they'd invited him in a half-hearted sort of way but, even if he'd been interested, there was no way he could have made it on his crutches, especially in the rain.

This morning, at any rate, the weather was fine, and as a cloud moved away from the sun, sharp rays of light found their way in through a few small clear patches in the windows, and the room was patchily but fiercely illuminated. What B saw was dirt. Not only on the windows themselves, but, suddenly, in sharp focus, he saw the dust, the stained walls, and the caked mud (and God knew what else) in the corners of the room. He thought he had cleaned the place, but as a summer-strong sunlight entered the room he for the first time saw his surroundings for what they were. *Show us our darkness.* B shrank back at the thought. He wasn't sure he wanted his darkness illumined. But he did want the sun.

With a brusque movement, he rose from his chair. Suddenly he resented with a passion all the protective dirt that kept the sun out. He wanted to scrub away the muck, clear a pathway for the light to pour into this sunless space, wanted to throw open the window and bask in the heat and light.

B knew that he must be horribly pale by now. The sun wasn't something he had taken much notice of, in general, except to keep out of it. As a fair-skinned lad, he burned easily. So he didn't get brown, but in his running days he had managed to acquire a healthy glow. When he cooked up this plan during those months in hospital, he had been so shut in a sunless world that this kind of deprivation hadn't occurred to him. How could he have been so short-sighted? As he looked out of the window, he saw the flash of sunlight on a passing car; he saw people in tee-shirts and shorts, strappy dresses and, oh God, seemingly bare legs. They were no longer hurrying to go anywhere, but pausing in groups, chatting and laughing. He could hear their voices, if not what they said. Just outside his window, a jogger was leaning against a lamp post, turning his face up to the sun. B was swamped with envy and desire. With all his grieving heart, B wanted to run again. He wanted the light and the warmth of the sun. And he wanted the life that depended on it.

B was surprised how tired he got. Living intensely in every moment took its toll. Not that he often managed it, but just the effort, trying to pay attention to every smallest detail: when he was washing up, for instance: watching the way the bubbles shifted ever so slightly but all the time, and the hissing sound as they did so. The circles of oil in the water, separated out.

And pain was an increasing problem. The stored-up prescribed painkillers had long since been consumed, and the over-the-counter remedies just didn't do the trick. Their lack of impact had a cumulative effect; sleep was harder to come by at night, and then he had to fight to stay awake during the day. There were times, in meditation, and on the very first instant of waking, when pain was absent, but it was otherwise as much a part of his physical being as its usual bodily functions. He had lived with it so long. It wasn't until he put weight on his leg that he could feel the full brunt of today's level of pain, or rather the level of pain for that time, as it varied even from one moment to another. It was extraordinary how he could get up twice in the night, and the levels of pain would be quite different. When he hadn't *done* anything, what determined it? Maybe he ran marathons in his sleep. Yeah, right. He hadn't ever run marathons, even in the days when he ran regularly. The idea of measuring the distance, let alone of competing, was alien to him. It would be to impose those usual sterile, target-driven inhibitions on the one activity that gave him freedom and kept him sane.

The continuous struggle was wearing him out and on some days he could not summon the energy to do his exercises. Sometimes B wondered how he was going to carry on: one day, he supposed, he simply wouldn't get up. A day would come when he would finally have had enough of the hourly struggle, the battle against pain, to keep to his routine, most of all to keep faith with his dream. What was the point? There was no future. He was kidding himself. He would just fade away, moulder in these dank and murky rooms.

His books on Buddhism taught not only that suffering is a central part of life, but that detachment from everything is a major part of the peaceful path. How B wished he could be detached from his pain. Or, rather, pains, for there were several different kinds. He tried to deflect his attention from teeth-gritting endurance by a kind of analysis. There were the localised stabbing pains around the pin sites, where the skin felt stretched, or had been knocked so that the pins cut into the muscle; there was the general complaint of the muscles, and the deep-down mind-numbing groaning bones themselves. He could almost hear them saying: *put us out of our misery.* Then there was the less acute but numbingly generalised ache of an enduring body. Permanently compensating for a damaged leg put his whole frame out of synch. Until now he had been rigorous about doing his exercises – stretching, flexing, keeping the muscles as supple as he could – but months of no proper exercise had wreaked havoc with his stamina and his strength.

He didn't know what he thought about death. He considered it from time to time, but hadn't come to any conclusion. Without personal experience there was nothing to help him. He'd had experience of others dying, had even got quite used to the idea when first Gran, then Jeff died. Then, of course, Dad and, last of all, Mother. But the death of others had brought him no fresh insights into his own. He wasn't afraid, except of the possibility of even greater pain in the process, but maybe his lack of fear was because it was not yet a present reality. Maybe in the event he would be terrified, but somehow he didn't think so. It was part of life, after all, as it was for the whole of creation. He wasn't too bothered. It might even be a relief.

B did not see the eremitic life as preparation for any life to come; he wasn't sure he believed in any such thing. Unlike those he thought of as real Buddhists, he didn't believe in reincarnation: that seemed too simplistic. Why would one come back in another body? But some sort of extended life for the spirit seemed to make sense. Most of all, that the elements of his body would dissolve back into the universe from which they had come. That sense of connection was fundamental. But his spirit? Soul? He couldn't see it simply disappearing, not because it was his, but because it was bigger than him. When he caught a glimpse of the stars, it was not only with a sense of awe at the hugeness, the distance, the millions of years that separated them, but also with a strange feeling of kinship. Stars had died so that he could exist. It was only right that on his death, his tiny body would make its own contribution.

There had been times as a teenager when B had wanted to die. For hours on end he had lain curled up in or on his bed, facing the wall. What was the point? He didn't fit in, wasn't liked, wasn't getting anywhere. What was there to live for? And then a little seed of disagreement would creep into his mind: what about his gran? And birds, and the green shoots of spring? But most of all, he kept going out of sheer bloody-mindedness. Damned if he was going to give into them, to give them the satisfaction of his demise. Those were dark times, but he was a mule, not a depressive, and that was what saw him through. He was angry, and that saved him.

And he had kept going because deep down he knew that there was something he had been born to achieve. He was waiting for his hero-self to come out, all colours blazing. Heroism was not something he had ever talked about – when had he talked about anything important and who would have listened? – but it was a concept he held deep within himself. Not in the loose sense that seemed to be bandied about on the radio and in the papers. *Falklands hero?* People trained to kill in a war that should never have started. *Olympic hero?* He could more relate to that one, but really his conception of heroism was of another kind, did not seem to fit the age into which he had been born.

B shook himself. In the end, he knew he would keep going. He had come here not to die, but to live!

Chapter 7

From childhood on, it had been B's practice, when he woke and before anything else, to put on his glasses. He always knew where they were. He took great care to put them somewhere memorable and safe. If he lost them, or Heaven forbid, trod on them, he too would be lost, blundering about the rooms like a blind bull. Putting them on was a move towards self-protection: he could not allow himself to be taken unawares. Without his glasses, he had felt less than: unprotected, a man of limited capability. But no longer. These days he deferred the moment, resting in a more centred space before putting on the first garment, as he saw it, of his external life. The change of practice was a sign of his expanded identity; it indicated his escape from fear into a self, however frail, in which he increasingly felt at home.

And so it was on this day. When he did, finally, reach for his specs and perch them on his nose and round his ears, he was startled to find in that new focus, just a few yards from his eyes, a small spider, maybe half a centimetre across, laboriously making its way on a shiny thread down from the ceiling. Yes, literally making its way. What an example of self-sufficiency. Alone, yes. Had he ever seen more than one spider at a time? A spider always seemed to be singular, doing its thing, making its way.

B would not have believed that he could fall in love with a spider. As a small child, he had seen himself as the saviour of little living things. Maybe it was because they too were small, and he could identify with their helplessness before the might of Mother's broom. But he'd long grown out of that allegiance. After years of hassle, he had gradually stopped wanting to grovel on the ground, muddying his knees and tearing his trousers. As he'd grown bigger, so his interest had shifted to bigger animals, and of course at the surgery he'd seen them at closer quarters, and his heart had been won.

His childish curiosity about little crawling creatures had evaporated as he grew older and had gradually been replaced by the attitude to insects of everyone he knew: that of disgust. Even when later in life he found a religion that affirmed the sanctity of all life, a faith which had at its centre a love for all living creatures, he had continued to struggle with creepy crawlies, trying to wish them well, but to wish them somewhere else. So, when he first arrived he was profoundly grateful that there was no trace of woodlice, silverfish or cockroaches in these rooms, or if there was, he'd been blissfully unaware.

But in recent days there had been a sea-change in his consciousness. Now he considered that the shift in his attitude as he got older hadn't been growing into anything; it had been a shrinking, a shrinking into conventional thinking. How he wished that his knees were up to grovelling nowadays, and that he had a garden to do it in. How he wished he'd done some smuggling into this place. But at the beginning he'd had no idea of the devastating creaturely emptiness here – barren, you might say literally, of creature comforts – and in any case when he came he'd have scoffed at the idea. It was only when he'd been living in freedom for a while that he'd been able to shrug off the overlay of prejudice, and recapture that small boy's spirit. He missed them now, these unsung companions, and on stormy nights, as in childhood, he lay in bed and worried about the little mammals, birds and, yes, insects cowering under the leaves.

Unlike his sister, who screamed if she found one in the bath, he'd never been afraid of spiders, at least the small ones, although he would not have invited their presence. But when he woke that morning and saw this little black creature caught in an arrow of sunlight, he was captivated. It seemed unusually early. Surely they only appeared in the autumn? He remembered a rather nutty old man in hospital who believed that spiders came as messengers: if they appeared, one had to pay attention. In this moment, recalling his childhood open-heartedness, he could almost believe it.

When he got up, B was careful not to disrupt the spider. When he straightened his bedclothes later in the morning, he half-expected to see it, but it had scurried away into some dark corner. A flower, a blackbird, and now a spider. It was as if life had entered his rooms at last, as if they were peopled. The presence of others became for the first time a palpable reality, a possibility, something to be welcomed, even – B did not like to admit it – something to be longed for. It was horribly unsettling.

At last the moment had come. It was the third and last set, and he had waited many weeks – months? – before allowing himself to broach what had to be the finest, the culmination of his work, for there would be no more. Before coming here he had managed to find some sand mandala kits. Until a few months ago, he'd never made a mandala himself, only seen it done by some Tibetan monks, but he had known that the profound process of the making – and, even more, the destruction – would enable him to enter a place of devotion, and practise mindfulness to a higher degree.

He had waited for what he calculated would be the new moon, the most propitious time for a new project. Anything begun now would grow into a greater fulfilment of new life. For the last few days he had eaten little and extended his meditation practice as a spiritual preparation, stilling his mind and opening his heart to allow the creative forces a space in which to enter. Even so, his physical heart beat faster as he unlatched the cupboard, gazed on the two urns that held the used sand, before lifting down all the necessary accoutrements. Walking with one crutch, he carried first the perspex sheet, then the funnel and guiding templates, to the square table in the corner of the room. Lastly came the tray that held the precious pots of pristine sand:

the five sacred colours of yellow, red, blue, green and white. The tray was heavy and hard to manage, but he clasped it firmly in his right hand, and limped slowly and precariously to the table, which had been wiped clean and left to dry in preparation. All distracting objects had been removed from what would be his sight line. He set the tray down on the centre of the table, returned to shut the cupboard door, then went for a pee. After carefully washing and drying his hands, he went back to the table. He stood for a while in front of the tray, a sense of anticipation both nervous and serene as he faced the beginning of the long and profound process. There would be no place for clumsiness in the piping of minute quantities of sand on to his board. It would take all his concentration.

A mandala represented for B the union of matter and spirit. Making one was a sacred act, an attempt to harmonise all the disparate elements in himself, and in the universe. He knew his own inadequacy, and didn't underestimate the challenge or the difficulty of the task. Although the design that he made was rarely balanced in a way he had initially intended, it usually had some sort of symmetry of its own. Accepting that the outcome was unknowable and uncontrollable brought him closer to an acceptance of the mystery at the heart of creation, and made him feel that even his small self might be part of it.

He stilled himself, closing his eyes, planting his feet on the ground, feeling the roots go down through the floor, through the lower storeys, into the earth beneath, and down to solid rock. He stood still for a while, breathing slowly. It was time. He opened his eyes, lifted the lids off the pots, and placed them carefully on the table.

As B reached towards the tub of white crushed gypsum sand, he thought he saw a black dot. No, yes, there it was. How did that get there? As he reached a finger in to remove it, it moved. It was alive; it was a creature! Desperately he fished in the sand which trickled into itself like water, covering every empty space, covering the creature. An ant? A fly? Hobbling back to fetch a mug, he used it to bale out larger quantities of the sand, and there, finally, was his little black spider, curled up now, and dead.

B lifted it out on a finger tip and laid it on the table. It was incomprehensible – and devastating. Just as a living creature had finally entered his sanctum, just as he had opened his heart to it, it was gone. It was also a sullying of the purity of the sand, the matter of his spiritual practice. How could he respond to this desecration? What did it mean? How would it affect the process of the next few days? Was it some kind of omen? He sank on to the chair, appalled.

He stayed sitting for a long time, head bowed, eyes closed, all idea of beginning the mandala dashed. Eventually, he pushed himself up, replaced the lids on the tubs, the tubs on the tray, and the tray in the cupboard. He returned to the chair, put his face in his hands, and tried to recover his composure. *Detach.* When he opened his eyes, the first image, the only object on the polished table, was the little black spot of the spider, the snuffed-out life. A little live creature and he had killed it. At the heart of his faith was the sanctity of life, and in the heart of his practice a creature had met its death.

That night he was clumsy. Shaken out of his fragile equanimity, he rushed the serving of his meal, and dropped some of his salad on the floor. Whereas in his former life he would have had no qualms about picking it up and eating it, from this floor there was no recovery. Gritting his teeth, he went to fetch his litter pick, painstakingly picked up each leaf from the floor and dropped them into the bin. The food was wasted. Yes, it was a little thing, but a symptom of a deeper malaise.

As a child, B had been frightened of the dark, not so much because of nameless demons that might have been lurking in the shadows, but because he feared that, having become invisible to the world, he might cease to exist. He didn't dare to explain his fears to anyone, but even a tentative request for a night light was greeted by *Nonsense, don't be so silly*. So, for many years, he had kept himself awake at night until he could no longer hold back his surrender. The belief in invisibility had lingered but he no longer feared it. Now that he saw himself as part of a greater reality, the dark had become his friend. He was visible only to himself anyway these days, and even that was less than before. Without either a glass mirror or the mirroring views of others there was very little of himself now that he could see: never his back or, more importantly, his face. If he almost crossed his eyes, he could see the tip of his nose; if he puffed out his cheeks, in and out, he was aware of a flesh-coloured anonymous fuzzy shape coming and going. But it was not his face, not really. B sometimes imagined what a visitor might find, and wondered whether he himself would blend into the background. Maybe he was beginning to disappear. He thought that a self-portrait might fade away at the edges, seep off the sides of the canvas.

Every evening, B longed for the moment when he could allow himself to rest in the comfort of his bed, the moment when he could let his ache-filled body sink into softness. And the moment when he could let go of even that bit of the self that he could see. In that lack of consciousness, he left both his pain and his troublesome self behind. He was no longer imprisoned by four walls but could imagine himself in the land of his dreams. No, not land – universe. The vast horizon of his dreams extended beyond any land he knew. He felt himself whirling out into infinite space.

Surprisingly, he didn't generally mind waking up. For a few magical moments the dream world and night-time reality lingered; briefly his consciousness was both within and without as awareness dawned of the existence of a new day.

Now that B was cut off from the natural world, he unexpectedly found solace in the sight of people going about their daily lives. He found himself more and more drawn to his peep holes, more and more drawn to the world beyond his refuge, from which he had so eagerly cut himself off. He found it increasingly hard to stick to his routine, craving sight of ordinary life, life as lived by others. The boy cycling up the street – look, no hands! The grey-haired man in shorts with a newspaper tucked under his arm, the woman in hat and coat weighed down by the plastic shopping bags hanging from either hand. The little man with a pork pie hat strutting along the road. Human beings. How had he not noticed the extraordinary variety of physical types, of people? Had he noticed anything?

Having spent much of his life avoiding other people, B was disturbed now to acknowledge how much he missed them. Not in terms of social interaction, which had nearly always been unsatisfactory, but just the awareness of others' activity, like a running accompaniment to his own life, a thread that ran parallel and occasionally crossed his own. He missed the sound of someone laughing or coughing or flushing the loo. He missed the whiff of the aftershave of a passer-by in the street, the touch of someone brushing against him in the lift. However little attention he had paid to human activity, it had always been *there*, and his life felt depleted without it. It was for that reason that he cared passionately about his daily "walks" as a last-ditch connection to the rest of the human race.

How astonishing it would be if his own presence were missed in a similar way. He knew that his family were likely to "miss" him, somewhat as a birthmark that has always been there, but he was talking about something broader than that. How would it be if instead of the interconnections with him which others had so obviously found irritating, even alien, the subtraction of his own daily activities had somehow caused a loss to the world at large? It was highly unlikely – there were enough people in the world – but metaphysically (*six syllables!*) there was some comfort in the thought.

Of course, there was no way he could suddenly open his window and shout out his presence to the street. But there was one person with whom he was already in contact, one person whom he could easily meet, and who would be glad to see him, and the idea of that possible meeting swelled in his mind to almost obsessive proportions. With a sense of shame, B began to stay awake even on nights when he knew Hamid was not due to come, listening for quiet steps on the stairs, the rustling of bags, and the sound of an envelope pushed under his door. When the sounds finally came, he stood with his ear to the door, almost holding his breath. He could hear the breathing of the other man as he placed the bags outside, could feel, almost smell, his presence. He had to fight with himself not to open the door. A mixture of pride and shyness stopped him. Hamid would be astonished. What would they say to each other? But, most of all, B was fearful that once opened, the door on his solitude would never close again. There would be no going back.

He was in awe of Hamid. How did a young educated man leave everything that he had known, come to live in a foreign country where his own language was not understood, and put up with such a barren and dangerous existence. Not only put up with it, but bear it with such grace. He was not only reliable but unfailingly courteous and kind. B was ashamed of his initial response – that this man could be useful. What he saw now was that this man was a teacher, a lesson in himself. What a gift that his own life should depend on such a man. To his dismay, B found that his cheeks were wet. What was the matter with him? Having avoided contact with others all his life, having sought this solitude, he now found himself unaccountably drawn to strangers. Maybe it was because they were strangers, because they were at a safe distance. He had no doubt that actual contact with them would be as awkward and uncomfortable as it had always been, but at this remove he realised for the first time the beauty of a human being.

After all the years of dreaming and planning, the months of adjustment, it was almost unbearable to acknowledge to himself that this was not enough. To begin with, there had been joy and excitement, an expansion into the undisturbed space and the growth of self-acceptance. The establishment of his routine and the physical challenges of the conditions had kept him occupied until boredom had set in. Coming through the boredom threshold had, he knew, been a milestone: in that process he had discovered something like peace of mind. He had felt a sense of belonging in his solitude. Why could he not have been content with that? For there was no denying that now it was simply not enough. Now that he had recovered himself, he felt that he had outgrown this space, felt almost as if his body were pressing against the walls, threatening to burst through into the street outside.

Some of it was purely physical. He was a young man, for God's sake, living the life of an old one. Yes, he did his exercises, but when had he last had any *exercise*? Felt his lungs and heart stretched? His whole body was in danger of atrophy: somehow he'd got to move it, use it, vent some of this physical energy.

He kept having to reassess his original impressions. He'd been wrong, for instance, about being part of this neighbourhood. How could he have thought it? Trees grew and shed their leaves, people went on their way, regardless of his attention. Unaware. Unwitting. Uncaring. And the stories he'd woven around them. They were pure fiction. And maybe the reality wasn't as innocent as he'd imagined. Who knew what was going on in that house opposite, and who was part of it? Watching others as they passed his windows each day, B wondered what lay behind their appearances. He also wondered how much he himself had been observed in the past, in his running, working, travelling on bus or train. He knew all about CCTV, but had there been secret watchers? Surely there had not been anything worth seeing in his mute and oh-so-private life. All the same, the possibility made him profoundly uneasy.

It had been the strength of his will that had kept B going, through the miseries of first childhood and then the accident, and now in carving out for himself an independent life. But now, to his terror, he felt it crumbling. His yearning for contact was threatening to undermine the edifice of protection that he had so carefully built around him. Surely hermits had occasionally given into temptation? Some of them, he seemed to remember, even accepted guests. But his solitude, he knew, was born of different roots from theirs. Did he dare to explore what had brought him here? To begin with, he knew, it had simply been an escape. For his own soul's salvation, he had been able to do no other. But there had been more than that. He wasn't clear about what it was but he felt he had been on some sort of a quest.

There was life out there, and he was not part of it. The newly confident "he" needed fulfilment in something beyond himself. And there was nothing he could do to make that happen.

In the emptiness B began to be aware of the voices. In the early days it had been as if Mother had pursued him from beyond the grave. He knew that the voice had often been hers although, having absorbed so much of it over the years, he was sometimes hard put to distinguish her voice from his own. But that voice had faded while he'd been living here, and now there were the others. He heard them mostly at night, just before going to sleep; sometimes they were indistinguishable from his dreams, and sometimes they kept him awake. But he wasn't disturbed by the fact that he heard them; they were often welcome company, usually not anything to do with him, but random conversations, sometimes odd words in other languages, as if they were from people passing by. Some were the voices of children, laughing and playing. They made him smile, and reminded him of Vicky. He found he missed her. There had been a solidarity between them, an unspoken companionship: they seemed at ease in each other's company – a rare thing, in his experience. But it was more than that: he seemed to find in himself a sort of yearning. Did he want kids, was that it? Could men be broody? Not much point if he was. Better not go there.

But more recently the voices were more distressing. They were pleading voices, voices of those living ghostly existences: Hamid's sister, Zahra, seemed to be there along with Aishe and her companions, begging for help. He couldn't miss Aishe's voice: high and clear with its enchantingly accented English. He wriggled in the confines of his sleeping bag. Why were they coming to him, these voices? What was he meant to do? At least he hadn't started seeing things as well – that would have been too much.

No, he didn't see things, but he began to be aware of a thickness of presence in the air. It wasn't just the voices that had entered his life: the place seemed strangely peopled: "haunted" was the word that came to him. But he could not have mistaken the untroubled welcome of these walls. If the place were haunted now, they were ghosts that had come with him.

He was appalled to find that even Annette crept into his consciousness. For all her faults, she did have an enviably sunny personality, even though its impact had dimmed a little – or maybe been re-directed – with marriage and motherhood. Others said she lit up the room and B, though unwilling to admit it, knew that he missed the warmth of that light. His life, though free of his sister's interference and more his own, was cooler without it. Even while disliking her, he felt the chill of separation.

Maybe he wasn't a hermit after all. Just a frightened little boy who had run away. The thought was not palatable. The hermit image, like that of the hero, was a rooted part of his identity. Those were the twin poles of his secret being that had held him together for all these years. Maybe to be a hermit required another dimension, a greater sense of the transcendent. Hermits prayed: that was what they did, what kept them sane – and he had nothing to pray to.

How could he have incarcerated himself in this way? It was true that before he came here he had also been hemmed in not only by his physical constraints, not only by the limitations of indoor living, but by the all-consuming need to escape before the others took him over completely. He had felt like an old man who had given himself up to the control of an enduring power of attorney. Get out before he lost his leg, his sense of self, his will to live. It had all been about getting out: he'd thought little about what he was getting into, and whatever he'd imagined that to be seemed now to be a mirage.

In that madcap flight he had cut himself off from the source of his reverence and his redemption. He had shut himself up in a barren box. How he wished to touch a living being. Even a leaf to stroke and to treasure, to trace its delicate veins and wonder at the subtlety of its finely shaded colour. He wanted to hold beauty in his hands. The invisible Hamid was his saviour in this, as in so much, his one tenuous link with the material world. The fruit that he brought from the market had been picked off its stem but still shone with life. It was not just for some abstract exercise of mindfulness that B caressed the skin of a plum, and rubbed it against his cheek, but an urgent need to feel the reality of creation, connect himself to beauty, be part of something. He was so alone.

Chapter 8

He could have so easily missed it. He'd noticed before that what matters is so often seen almost by accident: a little flash of activity while the world goes about its business. Pain had woken him, as it often did, but for once he did not go straight back to bed after peeing; he had no idea how far through the night it was, but he didn't feel sleepy. It was unusual for him to look through his peep holes in the early hours. Normally, to fall asleep again he needed to avoid light or stimulus of any kind. But this was the night of the full moon, and a glimpse of the moon was worth any degree of disturbance. Or so he thought. He was about to turn away from a dispiritingly overcast sky when the street lamp caught a flicker just at the corner of his eye.

The flicker was the opening of the back doors of a white van. It was parked outside the building site – at this time? – and there were two men standing at the rear. They were not in builders' day-glo gear, but in some sort of dark clothing. As he watched, he saw that they were getting something out, each of them taking an end. It looked a bit like a stretcher. All he could see on it was a kind of blanketed shape, and above it a white face, and streaming long black hair. What were they doing? Were they carrying a body into an empty building? The door into the building – the one marked "Site entrance. Hard hat area" – must have been open, because the first man was already moving out of sight and as the stretcher followed him into the darkness, B saw a white arm thrown up from the stretcher as if in appeal. The other man quickly slammed it down, and the rest of the little procession was engulfed. B peered into the darkness, but there was no movement. The night was still.

B stood still in shock. What on earth was going on? Had he imagined it? That was an empty house; it was a building site. Where could they be taking her? And why? She was obviously alive. Who was she? Remembering the other odd happenings that he'd witnessed over the months, he swung round from the window, his heart thumping. He had not imagined it. There were people in there, presumably she was not the first. Trembling, he limped round the room on his crutches, from one side to the other, and then into the bathroom and back, almost knocking into the basin as he turned himself round. For the first time in months, his peace of mind had completely deserted him; his inner stillness had been rocked.

What could he do? That had been an appeal, he was sure of it. And even if she didn't know it, he knew in his heart that the appeal had been for him. The other glimpses had been hints, signposts to this moment. He had waited a long time for this. This was personal: it was as if her outstretched hand had touched him into life. But how could he respond, from this, this *prison*? As he hobbled to and fro, he was for once unaware of any physical discomfort, aware only of the impact of this extraordinary happening, searching his heart and brain for some way forward.

- *No, there's nothing.*

- *But she...*

- *Nothing I can do.*

But even as he affirmed his helplessness, a seductive worm wriggled into his consciousness.

- *I could always...*

- *No, absolutely not. Not that. That would mean...*

The thought was terrifying, but it was a thought that would not go away. He knew it came from his core, and in the end he succumbed. Whatever it meant, he would do it. What he would have to do was to keep watch, and to wait. If by the morning she had not come out, he would know what to do. But, first, he had to be prepared.

Sheltering the beam of his torch with his hand, he found in the back of his cupboard the small cardboard box. Underneath the tennis balls, the jar of drawing pins and the jumble of other forgotten objects was the mobile phone that Annette had given him all those years ago, and which, in a tremulous hiatus of faith, he had thrown in there "just in case". He replaced the other objects in the box, and the box itself in the cupboard, and with the phone in his hand hobbled towards the window, where the light was better. He looked down at the chunky little machine, knowing the consequences of its use. For some time he leant against the wall, trying to gather the ragged edges of his self-possession. Then, hastily but deliberately, he pressed the top of the phone to switch it on.

And nothing happened. He tried again – nothing. Nothing happened no matter how many times he tried, using his nail and his other thumb. The feeling of relief was inescapable. There was nothing to be done, nothing to trigger the mayhem, all the forces with the power to uproot him from his precious existence. But at the same time his mind told him that the battery was flat, and that somewhere there was a charger. It had not been in the box. These days he would not have been so unmethodical, but then he had been untrained; he had been a novice. He finally found the charger in the other box, under his bed, and, before second thoughts could arrest the momentum, he plugged the phone in the charger into the socket on the skirting board. The inevitable process had begun.

He dragged a chair to the window, and settled down to watch. The peepholes were above his eye level now he was sitting down, but there were little blurry gaps further down the window, which made it possible for him to peer out. As he sat, he did not worry about falling asleep, nor about sleeplessness. Sleep was elusive on the best of nights and adrenalin would, he knew, sustain him through the vigil. There were probably only a few hours anyway until daylight. Then B would know. If they were going to bring her out, it would be at night. They would not risk being seen.

If he had slept, he knew he would have dreamt of knights on

chargers, a lady tied to a rock, like that painting he had seen, wringing her hands with distress. As it was, he could almost feel the breastplate on his chest, the warm horse's flanks between his thighs. He played what he'd seen over and over in his mind: a clear focused picture of the van, the dark shapes, the stretcher, the pale face, the hair and, most of all, the raised arm peremptorily pushed down before the group entered the darkness of the doorway. He tried to remember if there had been anything else, any other details, whether he had caught any other movement out of the corner of his eye. But all had been blanked out by the dark. That snapshot was all he had seen. He fought emotion, wishing with a portion of his heart that he'd been wrong, that he'd mistaken what he'd seen, that they would bring her out, that his life was not going to be shattered in the morning. But there was too a steely seed of heroism in his gut, a sense that this was the moment for which he'd been born.

In much the same way that Vicky's eyes had held his all those years ago at her christening, the raised arm of this unknown woman was a call: a cry from one outsider to another. As the street receded into stillness, its darkness lit only by the street lamp opposite, it was as if nothing had happened. But in his heart B knew that everything had happened. He found it hard to breathe, or to swallow. He bent over, completely overcome. His heart was not just breaking, it was dissolving – into blood, snot, tears, and terror. The iceberg that had held him together for all these years was melting.

And in that dissolution flowed a new understanding. In what he had imagined his fellow feeling for those thousands of hidden lives, he was deceived. His hidden life was his freedom; it had been his choice. People like Hamid had no choice and people like the young woman opposite, like others in that building who might have been kidnapped or trafficked, they were held *against their will*. All that self-pitying stuff about his childhood. When he considered the possible fate of this young woman, of the women whose stories Hamid had shared, he was overwhelmed with love and shame. Constrained? Imprisoned? Had he been beaten, starved or, God save him, raped? He felt sick at the thought.

Eventually, B subsided into an exhausted state that was almost passive: he entered into a waiting when his outward attention was balanced by a stillness within. It was a new sensation: as if he held the outer and the inner in his body, as if the two were in perfect balance. He sat still, in a place of quiet certainty.

Dawn came slowly, and in Technicolor. The largely overcast sky was lit up by streaks of orange and red. As they faded, the cloud cleared, revealing a sky of limpid blue. When daylight entered the room, B turned wearily from the beauty before him, pulled his bag from under the bed, and threw into it the possessions he had packed on that hopeful day before it all began. He retrieved the diminished wad of notes from under his mattress, left behind the jigsaws and, after a hesitation, the urns of sand. He could not carry them, really, and they had served their purpose: monks, after all, usually threw the sand into the sea.

From the drawer in the bedside table, he found the little plastic bag he had put there on that first night and, as if arming himself against the outer world, took out the little dental plate with its single tooth attached. After all this time, his teeth had closed a little round the gap, and he pushed it in with difficulty, disliking the unfamiliar thickness to the touch of his tongue. Then he took it out again. Sod them. Whatever he faced, he was going to face it as he was. No more pretence. No disguises. Not any more.

He went over to the charger, disconnected the phone, and then looked at its blank face. The phone was dead. The charger hadn't worked. It was all too old, decrepit. But then, he'd known, hadn't he, that some kind of remote assistance would not do it. This was personal. It called for a personal response. Whatever it cost him.

Today's letter, he remembered, was Q. No time to draw it now: q with its tail. **Q** a circle of grandeur carrying its own strong sword. Q, as he had seen it in a manuscript all those years ago, with a knight inside, the tail of the dragon forming the tail of the letter. He mouthed the words: quin-tess-en-tial, quiv-er-ing, qui-et, *quest*.

He washed and dressed carefully. He dug out a smarter sweater from the back of the drawer, and it sort of fitted. He had no idea how he looked, and he didn't want to know. He tore a page of paper from his notebook and wrote a note to Hamid: "When you come, I shall have gone. Please keep this week's supplies. Thank you for all you have done for me. Good luck. B." He wondered what Hamid would do, how he would manage. He took up the pen again and, with tears streaming down his face, added: "I owe my life to you. Goodbye, my dear friend." He took out an envelope and put a month's money in with the note.

B dabbed his eyes, brushed his hair and combed his beard. He left the bag on his bed, as he had left it on that other bed all that time ago, reached for his crutches, and went over to the front door. He pushed back the old bolt at the bottom and unlocked the Chubb. He pinned the envelope to the outside of the door in the well-worn hole and stood on the threshold, bracing himself. He hobbled across the dark landing, put one crutch under his arm, took a firm grip on the other, grasped the banister with his free hand, and began his slow descent.

At Roundfire we publish great stories. We lean towards the spiritual and thought-provoking. But whether it's literary or popular, a gentle tale or a pulsating thriller, the connecting theme in all Roundfire fiction titles is that once you pick them up you won't want to put them down.